Evie

I am dead inside.

I don't know when I died. I can't remember an exact time, or point to a precise moment when the lights went out. It wasn't like someone had flicked the switch off and I had ceased to exist. My death had crept up on me slowly, had deceived me, gradually seeping into my skin one molecule at a time. I had no way of fighting it because I didn't know it was happening.

I hadn't seen it coming.

And now it was too late.

It (whatever it was, I didn't know) had eaten me alive like a parasite, had crept into my bloodstream, had taken me over until I felt nothing.

Nothing; like lying on your arm in the middle of the night and stopping the blood flow so that, when you finally wake, the arm is still there but feeling dead and detached, like it doesn't belong to you.

Josh

Death was coming.

I could hear Her rasping voice calling to me from the never-ending darkness.

Her scent - a pungent cocktail of soil, ammonia and lavender - was tumbling around me like a heavy veil of mourning.

But She didn't scare me.

I knew Her too well.

I ignored the violent curses she spat at me; She knew it was too late, she knew that I would betray Her and there was nothing that She could do to stop me.

I was going to save the girl destined to die, even if that meant I would lose my life in return.

I stepped back into the shadows - back into my realm - and continued to observe the girl sitting on the stone bridge, her legs dangling over the edge.

A clock began to strike twelve.

The girl slipped off her coat and clambered unsteadily onto the side of the bridge.

I waited for the moment the girl jumped.

The moment I would save her and my life would be lost.

Forever.

Evie

I exhaled, and watched as my breath turned to ice. The beauty of it always amazed me, like thousands of sparkling diamonds falling from the sky, bursting with memories of my father and those bitterly cold walks to school as we pretended to be dragons or trains. But I couldn't linger too long on those memories, they were as bitter as they were sweet, so I pushed them away, locked them deep inside me, alongside my tears.

I took another swig of vodka. I hated vodka, but it was all I could find to numb what was left of my already deadened senses.

Somewhere in the distance, beneath the thick veil of fog, a church bell began to strike twelve. My stomach lurched with anticipation. I took one last mouthful of vodka and placed the half-drunk bottle on the edge of the bridge; a glass gravestone, a marker, a reminder that I once was here, that I had once lived. I slipped off my coat and placed it next to the bottle. The skin on my arms prickled with goose bumps, but I didn't feel cold.

I scrambled clumsily onto the side of the Old Bridge, and counted the strikes of the bell. I couldn't miss my cue, not tonight. This one time I would do something right, perhaps for the first time, the only time, in my life.

It was a beautiful night to die, the spectral fog making it feel like the souls of those who had gone before were gathering around me, welcoming me into the next life. In the distance I could just make out the spiral of St. John's piercing through the fog's cold embrace. And I remembered my father, lying cold in its cemetery, beneath the frozen ground and out of reach, under a de-robed oak tree, its branches outstretched like a guardian angel.

Soon, I would be with him again.

A willow grieved on the river bank, its trunk bent double under the weight of the hoar frost that was clinging to everything like a second skin. A stray firework exploded in the distance, staining the fog with a diluted splash of red.

Strike nine.

I edged forwards, my heartbeat quickening as the taste of freedom opened up as a promise before me. Soon I would be free of life and the dark and heavy burden that I struggled to carry, like Atlas under the weight of the world. It had seeped through my skin like a morphine drip, drop by invisible drop, paralysing my heart, stripping me of feeling.

Suicide was just the end of my body being on earth; my soul, I knew, had abandoned me long ago and was already floating in the Waters of Forgetfulness on the Other Side.

Strike twelve.

A cacophony of fireworks erupted in the sky as drunken revellers screeched Auld Lang Syne.

And I let myself fall.

Into the water.

Crashing through the ice and into black.

The numbness inside me shattered with the ice, little particles of pain breaking free, and floating around me like snowflakes, beautiful but deadly when they merged together. Darkness engulfed me, the putrid, icy water pulling me down into its sanctuary and I heard the sweet voice of death calling my name.

At last, I was free.

Josh

I could feel Evie's life force slipping away as she sank under the fractured ice, it was calling to me, pleading with me to take it, to release it.

And I should have.

But instead, I plunged into the black water after her.

Evie was hanging in the water like a crucifix, millions of tiny bubbles dissipating around her; her life slipping away into nothingness.

As an Angel of Death, I remove the dying person's pain, and wash them clean, before I sever the thread that binds them to this life. I bear that pain, take their life stories from them, to prepare them for their onward journey into the Afterlife.

Not this time.

I flung my arms around her, and as we touched, images of her life flowed through me like a movie. Some were more vivid than others - her first cry as she was born to the world, her father taking her out on her first bike, his warm smile as he read bedtime stories to her, his last breath, the black funeral cars, the dark feelings that possessed her - and all of them cut me to the bone.

I pulled Evie closer to me, battling the leaden fingers of her pain as they wrapped themselves around me. They were trying to drag me down into that dark place in which she lived, they wanted to hold me prisoner until Evie was dead and I would have no other choice than to sever her soul and set it free.

Despite the heaviness invading my heart, I clung onto her and flew upwards, crashing out of the ice and into the blanketed world beyond.

She looked like a porcelain doll as I lay her down on the frozen embankment, her eyes closed, her heart barely beating. With the tip of my thumb I brushed away the matted hair from her face and then I kissed her.

And with that kiss I gave her back her soul.

And offered my life to Death in return.

Delicate threads of sparkling anima travelled through her body with the blood in her veins, winding their way to her almost dead heart. At the same time I returned her memories, her life story back to her, trying to hold onto the sorrow that had hijacked her existence, knowing I would bear it for a thousand lifetimes rather than see her suffer it again. But it was stubborn and cruel, and I couldn't hold onto it, nor stem the tide, and it rushed back into her.

A few ghostly images remained within me (probably from the darkest recesses of Evie's psyche), dancing upon the surface of my mind before they too vanished, almost like they'd never existed at all. They were memories that didn't make sense to me, that didn't seem to fit into her life - small glimpses of parted lips and naked flesh under a moonlit sky - but they were like snow on the ocean and in a matter of seconds they were gone, leaving only confusion and an inexplicable, aching hunger in their wake.

But I had no time to grieve their loss as Death, hissing and spitting, grabbed me by the hair and snatched me away from Evie. She spun me around and flung me to the ground. Agonising pain became master of my body. A silent scream uncoiled from my mouth.

I was to die beside the frozen river, not knowing if I had done enough to save Evie.

But Death did not take me.

Death is cruel and vicious and She wanted me to pay for my disloyalty, so She left me, broken and bruised, on the riverbank to die. Alone. A slow and painful death.

The sound of laughter drifted towards me, filtering through the thick curtain of fog. I had to get away, couldn't let whoever it was find me. I dragged myself into the brush and debris beneath the bridge, my feathers, tearing from my broken wings, left a snaking trail of black; a dark stain on the landscape. I rolled into a ball under the bridge, curling my arms around me to stop the trembling, but fear is a strong mistress and it took hold quickly, travelling through my body like cracks over ice.

I faintly remembered feeling something like it before, a long time ago. I drew no comfort from its familiarity.

There was nothing I could do but close my eyes and let Death take me when She was ready.

I heard my name being gently called through the darkness. There was a small flickering light in the distance - the place from where my name was being whispered - and I swam towards it, knowing that that was where I needed to be.

My eyes snapped open. I was lying naked on the hard ground, my body shaking from the icy cold biting into my skin. The harsh smell of burnt sulphur and charcoal hung on the air, and somewhere beyond the heavy cloud, the day was beginning to break. The bridge arched above me, oozing with emerald green lichen and centuries of dirt, the white-carpeted water, that usually rushed at its feet, lying still and silent beneath it. I saw the trail of black feathers twisting their way across the tow path, my feathers, bent and twisted like broken bones, and I remembered.

Evie.

I tried to stand but my legs were heavy, my body strange; blood throbbed in my veins - I could hear it pounding in my ears - and life pulsed through my body like electricity, animating every nerve and muscle. I stumbled backwards and pain stabbed my foot. I looked down; the jagged edge of a broken bottle protruded from the side of my heel, and my crimson blood was leaching into the mud from the wound.

But as an Angel of Death - an Immortal - I shouldn't have bled.

I leaned back against the arch of the bridge and slowly pulled the shard out of my foot, my own warm blood smearing my fingers.

I wanted to vomit.

I threw the fragment of glass to the ground, watching closely as the deep cut knitted back together and healed in front of me.

My ribcage seemed to constrict around my lungs, pushing my heart into my throat as the truth became clear.

I was no longer an immortal.

But I was not a mortal either.

Because no mortal would heal that quickly.

I was a bizarre mixture of the two - a freak - bleeding and weak, Death holding my life in the palm of her hands.

I didn't know how long I had left before She destroyed me, before I crumbled into oblivion - nothing more than dust on the breeze, destined to be absorbed back into the stars in which God had forged us - but I needed to find Evie before Death claimed me. I needed to see her one last time.

I knew she was alive. I could feel it, could feel her heart gently thrumming with mine.

But, despite my pleading and my aching need to see her, I didn't even make it off the tow path.

A grey cloud began to fall over my vision. I struggled to stay on my feet, clinging on to the trunk of a willow until my fingers bled, until my muscles roared with pain. I fought hard against Death's attack, and held onto life with everything I had, my mind oscillating between this world and the next, as I battled Her attempts to drag me back to the Other Side.

But finally, I lost the battle and Death's veil descended upon me.

I lost my grip on life.

Evie

An explosion went off in my head.

No, not an explosion, but a whole bloody war.

Bright daylight was imposing itself into my consciousness, its cold fingers trying hard to pry my eyes open, to make me face the world.

There was another explosion, but this time it wasn't in my head, but from somewhere out there, outside of me. In my mind, the bit that hovers between sleep and waking up, I pictured a war plane releasing a bomb before it moved off, circling in preparation for another strike. I knew it was going to come back, that it was just waiting for the right moment to attack again.

As I hurtled towards reality, other images surfaced from the darkest corners of my mind; of water, bitter and cold and black, trying to claw me down into its murky depths, the darkness punctuated by tiny shards of ice suspended around me like frozen angels.

Was I dead?

No.

The demonic beast - my torment - lived, and he was wriggling inside me, picking at my old wounds with his knife. A silent scream erupted from my lips, my body juddered as the realisation hit me; I couldn't even get my own death right.

I didn't deserve to live.

I didn't want to live. Not if I had to drag the beast around with me. I was so tired of carrying him around.

'Evelyn! Evelyn!'

My eyes flew open and I bolted upright in bed.

'Evelyn! Are you still in bed?'

It was Celia, my aunt, screaming like a banshee from downstairs; the war plane attacking me in my sleep.

Didn't she have anything better to do other than coming here to make my life even more of a misery?

Why couldn't she just leave me alone?

Alive. Having to deal with this shit.

My heart was rolling over in my chest and I couldn't breathe; I was suffocating.

Celia wasn't going to see me like this - over my dead body - I wouldn't let her have the satisfaction of knowing how low I'd fallen, of what I'd become, of what I'd very nearly done. And failed.

A failure. Yeah, that summed me up completely.

'Coming!' My voice was gravelly, my throat raw, like it was coated in tiny shards of glass.

I took a deep breath and hauled myself off the bed, catching sight of my reflection in the mirror on the wardrobe door. I stood still and took in the horror of what the mirror reflected back. Who was it that stared back at me? I didn't recognise her.

I felt sick.

'Evelyn!' shrieked Celia.

'Shit! Crap! Shit!' I cursed, coming back to reality. I run one hand through my hair trying to smooth the bird's nest that had taken up residence there, whilst the other frantically rubbed at the thick black mascara smudged over my face.

'Evelyn! Are you coming, or what?'

'Yeah, hang on,' I shouted back, 'I'm coming...Just give me a sec!' I peeled off my dirty blue tee-shirt, which had stuck to me like a second skin, and grabbed a cleaner looking one off the floor. It smelt okay, better than I did, so I pulled it on and then snatched a pair of grey tracksuit bottoms from my chair. I turned quickly to leave but stumbled as dizziness screwed with my vision.

I leaned up the wardrobe door for support, hoping the storm would pass quickly. My head was pounding, like the whole of the road works on the motorway had been crammed into it and all the men in hi-vis jackets were now using their pneumatic drills on my brain.

Slowly, the dizzying swirls of psychedelic colour in my mind subsided, leaving behind a heavy curtain of fog, and the feeling of nausea sloshing around in my stomach. There was a rancid smell in the air, like something had died, been buried and then been dug up again. The bed was damp and smothered in dirt, like it had been the thing that had died.

Beside the bed lay a pile of stinking wet clothes; my clothes, the clothes I'd jumped in. A single black feather lay on top of the pile, its rachis bent awkwardly like a broken leg, the barbs clumped together with mud.

Broken, like me.

I dived out of the room, not knowing what I would say to Celia about my appearance, my only hope was to wing it and hope I sounded convincing. I ran down the stairs and into the living room to find Celia shovelling beer bottles and pizza boxes into a black bin liner.

Yep, I'd got a lot of explaining to do.

'What the hell,' she screeched, 'has been going on here?' She looked up at me, her nose all wrinkled up like a bulldog, 'God you look like shit! And you don't smell much better either!'

Thanks, I said, but only in my head. I couldn't deal with the wrath of Celia, not today.

'Doesn't take a genius to work out what you were up to last night, does it?'

But I didn't have time to answer before she was ranting again.

'Trust you to get up to no good as soon as Cassie's back is turned. As if she hasn't got enough on her plate already, without this. Care to explain?' she said, turning to look at me, one pencilled eyebrow cocked high, her arms folded across her chest.

I looked around at the rubbish. I didn't remember any of it. I didn't even know how I'd got home. I scrambled around for words, for something, anything to tell her. But words failed me. I stared at her eyebrows instead; the raised one was wonky and thicker that the other eye, like she'd been drawn by a child. Why do people do that? Pencil in their eyebrows?

'Have a party did we? Of all the stupid things to do!'

'Sorry,' I mumbled. A party? I bit the inside of my lip so hard that I could taste blood in my mouth.

'Sorry?' screeched Celia, dropping the bin liner and swooping over to me like a red bird of prey. She stopped a centimetre from my face, so close that I felt her toothpaste breath on my skin. 'How much did you have to drink?' she said, grabbing my chin and forcing it upwards.

'Only a little bit-'

'It looks like you had a lot more than just a little bit.'

If only you knew the truth. 'Okay,' I sighed, wrestling my chin from her hand, 'I had quite a bit. It was New Year's Eve.'

Celia's green eyes narrowed. She let out a whistle of disapproval. 'Go and make me a coffee, two sugars.'

I was frozen to the spot, mesmerised by her terrible eyebrows. Well, not her eyebrows exactly, but I knew if I stopped concentrating on them I might have to start thinking about what exactly had happened. Stuff that I couldn't remember. Or didn't want to remember. Either way, it wasn't looking good.

'Coffee. Now, not tomorrow!'

'Okay!' I hissed back, forcing myself to move, feeling the nasty, stinking thoughts begin to circle in my mind, waiting to pick the bones of my anxieties clean. I dragged my sorry ass into the kitchen and switched the kettle on, grabbing a mug from the holder.

The last thing I could remember was jumping from the Old Bridge.

How did I get home?

Who was in my house last night?

Who put me to bed?

I picked up the sugar canister and noticed that my hand was trembling.

Sugar. How many did Celia take?

Who got me undressed?

No. I wasn't going to think about that.

My stomach rolled over. Did they only get me undressed?

I couldn't think properly, the curtain of fog that had fallen over my mind was now falling clumsily over over my whole body, covering everything, making things too hazy, too jumbled to see clearly.

The kettle bubbled rapidly, clicking off, dragging me back into the present. I picked the kettle up with a shaky hand and began to pour boiling water into the mug.

'For God's sake!' screeched Celia, as she swept into the kitchen, 'I asked for coffee. Jesus Evelyn, you can't even get that right!'

I flinched and boiling water sloshed over the side of the mug, onto the worktop and my hand. I dropped the kettle on to the counter, shocked, not by the pain, but by the urge to cry. I thought my tears had dried up long ago. I bit them back. I would not cry in front of Celia. I'd promised myself I would not cry in front of anyone.

'Forget it,' she shrieked, 'Carl's just texted me. I've got to go. Do yourself a favour, sober up and then clean this place up. I'll be back in a couple of days and it better be clean by then, ok? I don't want Cassie coming back to this, she's been through enough crap without dealing with this.'

I nodded, my back still turned towards her. I clung to the worktop, my knuckles white as I held myself up, just waiting for that precious moment when I would be alone.

The throbbing in my hand bit deeper.

The front door slammed shut.

I raised my hand to my eyes, studying it like it was some alien specimen in a jar. My hand was on fire and yet, although I was in pain, it didn't feel like it belonged to me. I wasn't used to feeling, I wasn't used to pain.

It was an almost beautiful feeling.

A battle was raging inside me; a fight between wanting the pain and feeling alive or succumbing to the numbness, the lack of feeling, that usually lived inside me.

I plunged my hand under the cold water tap and the pain swirled down the plughole.

Numb was winning after all.

I went back to playing dead.

There was nothing inside me. Nothing at all. Just an empty hole.

Tears rolled down my cheeks. A torrent of liquid pain.

I was crying for the pain in my hand, the pain that refused to be felt in my head, that my heart was yearning to feel.

I fell head first into the great swirling abyss, and into the demonic beast's lair. He had me in his claws, forcing me down onto the cold stone tiles. I lay there sobbing, unable to feel the cold seeping into my skin.

I was stone.

Josh

The darkness was never ending, a heavy funeral shroud pulling me down into its depths of despair, but I wouldn't let it take my mind, I couldn't let it claim me.

I kept my mind alive with thoughts of Evie, re-imagining our first kiss. Our only kiss.

I didn't know how long I'd been falling through that unforgiving darkness, with those thoughts and images orbiting around my mind like the planets, when the first glimmers of another existence, another place, appeared in the depths of the chaos like a new born star. At first it was a flicker, like the flame of a church candle in the wilderness and then it burned so brightly that it blinded me.

A beautiful voice called to me through the darkness, but although I recognised it, it didn't bring me comfort at all.

For this was the voice of Death.

And Death has three faces; which one would She reveal to me this time?

Slowly the veil of darkness lifted. I was lying naked on a grey flagstone floor, my wings, now unfurled, twisted awkwardly behind me.

Crumbling limestone columns ran either side of me, struggling to bear the weight of the vaulted roof above. The stars of Heaven sparkled through the fragmented ceiling, illuminating the statues of hooded angels, shimmering like ghosts, at the base of each column, their hands clasped in silent prayer.

This was the entrance to Death's domain, The Portico of a Thousand Angels, which crossed the murky waters of the Styx. The foul stench of the river - rotting flesh and stagnant water - clawed its way into my nostrils, a painful reminder that I was now half human, and weak.

'Rise!' Death ordered. Her voice cut through me like Heaven's Will, the angelic dagger that I always kept by my side to sever the souls of the dead.

Unseen hands pulled me up, forcing me to stand. I felt Her eyes watching me, felt them burning my skin although I could not see Her.

'Josh Winters.'

'My Lady,' I replied, bowing low, as is custom when addressing those angels of the First Sphere.

'You have been very, very busy.'

The gentleness of her tone hid the threat lurking behind Her words. The air was tight and heavy; a storm was building, a tornado twisting furiously on the horizon, and I knew it was going to tear straight through me.

'You have interfered in things which do not concern you.'

The fine fingers of a breeze stirred my hair, making me shudder, but I knew this was no breeze, but Death Herself.

'I hope,' She said, in little more than a whisper, 'she was worth it.'

Unseen lips brushed against my cheek and my body automatically reacted; my breathing became shallow, my pulse quickened as a strange heat coursed through me. My head fell forwards in shame.

'Mmmm, she smells divine; like amaranth, cherry blossom and white roses drowning in a sea of angel's tears.' She bit out the last few words like they were poison. 'She has affected you deeply; she has been under your skin for a very long time.'

I stood still and silent, like the statues lining the portico.

She continued. 'Will you not speak to your Mistress Josh, will you not dispute this or even plead for your life?'

'Why? My fate's already been decided.'

'Even now you think about her.'

'She's always in my mind.'

'I find it curious that, one that should not feel at all, loves so deeply.'

Death let her cloak of invisibility fall to the ground and stepped into the light. She was breathtakingly beautiful, glowing like the stars in the night's sky, her porcelain skin flawless.

'But what happens when I take your life Josh? Who will be there to save her then?'

Her noxious words hit their target, falling hard into the pit of my stomach, a lead coffin dropped into its burial pit. She knew every part of me, every weakness. There was no place to hide.

'You have upset the balance of things and now your life is forfeit. You have sacrificed your life for hers, and yet, she still might try and take her own life again. Such a waste, don't you think?'

Death swept in front of me, taking my chin in her delicate hand, forcing me to look into her eyes. A smirk played across her lips. 'Tears Josh?' she mocked, 'for a mortal soul?'

I wrestled my face from her hand.

'Does it hurt Josh? Does it feel as though your heart has been torn in two?' She ran Her hand over my cheek, its iciness biting deep into my skin. 'This is what happens when you meddle in matters that do not concern you.'

I couldn't reply; there were no more words left.

'Is it too much? Shall I end it now?'

She moved behind me and wrapped her frigid arms around my body, sheathing me in Her darkness. I felt the touch of Her wintry lips on the back of my head.

This was it. I was ready to die.

'No?' She whispered, 'Do you still cling on to the thought of her?' She let her arms fall from me. 'Would you like to see her again?'

'What do you want from me? Just kill me.'

Death now stood before me, her white gown swelling around her like waves in a storm. 'Do not be so bold as to question my authority!' She shrieked, although Her lips didn't move.

I was close to my end. For a few moments Her destructive face was clearly visible beneath Her porcelain skin, its surface now lined with fine but jagged cracks.

'If you like mortals so much,' She hissed, pointing Her finger at me, 'you can become one!'

Pain ripped through me as I was forced forwards onto my knees and onto the cold ground. Like a butterfly in a cruel boy's hands, my wings were forced open. The grey floor turned red as She plucked out my feathers. They fell, one by bloody one, like black tears.

The pain consumed me, making me beg, with words unspoken, for it to end.

Death finished stripping my wings bare, then stood up, towering over me with Her bloodied hands. 'Do not defy me again Josh,' she said, softly. She held up Her hands to show me the blood, 'Now look what you've made me do!' She sighed, wiping Her bloodied hands on her gown.

I couldn't move, fixed to the floor with fear and pain, a bloody, trembling mess.

'There is a way,' She said, stooping down to me, 'you can see her again, make sure she's alright.' She took my hand in Hers and gently raised me up.

I could barely stand, my legs were shaky, my skin clammy with blood and sweat.

'What? What sick game are you playing?' I asked, barely able to form the words.

'This is no game Josh, of that, I can assure you. You can go back and spend some more time with her.'

'Why? Why would you let me do that?' She saw the spark of hope dance across my eyes, heard the breath catch in my throat and She knew She had me in the palms of her hands.

'Of course, in return, you must do something for me...'

My fate was sealed. She had me caught in Her trap.

'What...what do I have to do?'

'Nothing too complicated. I only need you to find Hyperion, he seems to have disappeared.'

'Hyperion?'

Death nodded. 'Find him and remind him of his obligations here.' She turned and glided over to the edge of the Portico. 'Do you think you can manage that?' She said, looking out over the stinking waters of the Styx.

'But surely The Virtues know where he is?' I asked after Her.

'No, they are having trouble tuning in to his celestial music, something seems to be interfering with their instruments, and as you owe me...'

'But if the Virtues can't find him?' I asked, hobbling over to Her, my body still shaking with the memory of pain. I looked at the Styx as it boiled and whirled underneath the Portico, dragging with it the broken carcasses of ancient oaks and yews. In the distance, the twisted ruins of ancient temples lamented under the black sky, the roiling mist disfiguring their broken beauty.

'You'll find a way, I'm sure.' She held up a square of folded card, but did not look at me. 'This might be a good place to start. Hyperion was seen there, only a few days ago.'

I took the cream card in my hand but didn't open it.

'There are certain conditions, of course.'

'Conditions?' I looked up but She had already gone, absorbed back into the Never-ending darkness.

'Yes,' She said, from deep within it, 'your reprieve has certain caveats attached to it. You must never tell your mortal that you saved her the night she tried to take her own life-'

'But-'

'SILENCE!' screeched Death, as the stars seemed to snuff out, taking with them whatever light was left in the portico, 'You do not get to negotiate with me Josh! You can choose how you spend your time with her, but be warned, every second you spend in her presence will be filled with pain. You will feel like you are being pierced with a thousand swords every time you touch her. This is the punishment you must endure for your betrayal.'

'But-' I couldn't finish, the words stuck in my mouth as pain crippled me once more. My shoulder blades felt like they were being torn out as wings burst from my back, heavy and sticky and new-born. These new cumbersome wings, as black as Her darkness, pulled me backwards as they unfurled. They weren't mine, and felt strange, as though they belonged to another and I was just borrowing them.

'What...is...happening...to...me?'

'Oh,' mocked Death, 'did I forget to tell you that bit?' She cackled from somewhere deep inside the eternal darkness.

I shuddered as Her coldness attacked my burning body.

'From now on your wings will be hidden. If you need them, they will come, but not without causing you pain like you have never felt before.'

My vision blurred as the pain intensified, Her darkness closing around me. Defeated, I let it take me, let it soothe my pain.

Josh

I'd lain in the comforting arms of the dark for what seemed like an eternity before light imposed herself upon me, her long golden fingers caressing me like a long lost lover. My trembling body ached in a way that only a body that had been truly crippled with pain could ache, the memory of it held deep within my muscles.

I opened my eyes slowly, allowing them to adjust to the light. I was lying on frozen dirt, the roots of a gnarled oak tree meandering around me like snakes, rough and hard and smothered in moss. I dragged myself off the floor, feeling grateful that Death hadn't left me completely naked, but had clothed me in black again, my dagger, Heaven's Will, still safely at my side. Not that anyone would see me - I was sure of that - even as a freak, Death would make sure I was concealed by the elements when I needed it.

Across from me, about thirty metres to the right, I could make out Evie's house, its white hoar-capped roof illuminated by the low morning sunshine. It almost felt like I hadn't been away at all, and yet, I knew time had passed;

I felt it in the throbbing of my bones and the aching of my limbs.

I looked down at the folded card in my hand and then back to Evie's house. I knew why Death had left me here, but it didn't matter, I would not use my charms on Evie, even if it meant never being with her. Instead, I would wait it out - however long it took - just to see her one last time.

Then, and only then, I would face whatever torture awaited me.

The sun had fallen deep into the western horizon before I caught a glimpse of her. She emerged from the house under a pile of bags, and although my desire burned within me, I silently said goodbye to the girl I loved, the girl who would never know I existed. I would never come back, whatever Death thought.

Tendrils of physical pain uncoiled inside me, clawing their way into my heart.

I would never be close to her, would never touch her again.

Ever.

I turned away from her for the last time and unfolded the card in my hand. The spidery words on the card directed me to an address in Harlem, New York.

And without looking back, I took flight into the evening sky.

Evie

 I woke the next day in my own bed, although I couldn't remember dragging myself off the kitchen floor, nor staggering up the stairs. There seemed to be great chunks of my life recently that I couldn't remember, that were a complete mystery to me.

But the demonic beast, that sapped my strength and devoured my feelings, was always present, but on some days I found the courage to fight back, to push those dark thoughts and feelings back deep within me. These days were a safe harbour in miles and miles of stormy ocean, a gift that had no rhyme or reason.

Today was such a gift, although it shouldn't have been - not after my "accident" - but I didn't question it, just clung onto it with trembling hands.

I showered, pulled on fresh underwear, a pair of jeans and a pink Hello Kitty tee-shirt. My hand was a little sore and red where I'd spilt the water on it but nothing too serious. I grabbed the first aid box from the bathroom, emptied the dregs of the antiseptic cream over it and bandaged it up before I made my way downstairs. I went straight into the kitchen - avoiding the chaos in the living room - and popped a pod in the coffee machine. The delicious smell of coffee infused the air as I rifled through the cupboards trying to find something not passed its sell-by-date for breakfast.

Cassie hadn't bothered to shop before she went on holiday on New Year's Eve and I hadn't because there wasn't much point, not when I didn't plan on being around.

My mind wandered back to that night, on the Old Bridge, but I resisted the temptation to linger there. Instead, I rejected those thoughts, forcing them back inside.

All I could find was a strawberry pop tart a month out-of-date, but it looked half edible so I ate it, before gulping down my coffee. Then I turned my attention to cleaning. I pulled my hair into a pony-tail and opened the door to the living room.

The stench of half-eaten pizza and stale beer was disgusting. I turned on my docked iPod and the Foo Fighters blasted out. Everlong, the last song I'd listened to before I...

I switched it up loud and turned my attention to the bottles of Bud and Becks that decorated the coffee table.

I shoved everything into bin liners and then vacuumed and dusted. By the time I had finished, the room was spotless, smelling only of polish and floral air freshener with no hint of whatever had happened in there. Not that I could remember any of it.

I raced upstairs - trying to keep myself busy, trying to ignore the beast in my gut, poking at my insecurities and anxieties - and threw my bedroom windows open wide. I grabbed the dirty bed clothes and felt something small fall from the pile. It hit my foot and then rolled onto the floor. I dropped the washing down on the edge of the bed and picked it up. It was a diamond earring about the size of a pin head.

I sat down on the edge of the mattress, twirling the square diamond in my hand. It wasn't mine, I knew that for sure, but whose was it?

There was only one person I knew that wore earrings as big and expensive as this.

Dexter.

My heart jumped.

Had he brought me back here?

I pictured his big brown eyes shining before me, imagined him saving me, bringing me home. Maybe he was the reason I wasn't lying at the bottom of the river.

Maybe he actually cared.

And for the first time, in a very long time, I let myself believe.

Evie

 The last few days of the Christmas holiday passed by without me even noticing. Time had a habit of doing that to me.

The sun had disappeared again, eaten by the grey clouds hanging low in the sky, heavy with the promise of rain or snow.

I left for school, freezing in my purple hoodie. I'd briefly thought about going back to the Old Bridge, to see if my coat was still there, but it seemed so sick and twisted, like going to visit the scene of a crime, so I dismissed the idea and decided to freeze instead. I'd just have to find my other one, which was probably screwed up somewhere at the bottom of my wardrobe.

I boarded the number three bus clutching the diamond earring that I'd found in my room.

I'd decided that when I got the first opportunity I was going to give it back to Dexter, and I was going to ask him all the questions that had been swimming around in my head since I'd found it.

I needed to know why he'd saved me because it had to mean something. Didn't it?

It had to mean my life meant something.

I stepped off the bus holding the earring so tightly that I could feel it cutting into the palm of my hand, a perfect replica etched in red upon my skin. I wrapped my arms around my chest; the cold penetrated my bones far too easily these days, and it had only gotten worst since my dip in the river. I hurried across the staff car park towards the student entrance of Riverside Academy and the warmth of the Reception and cafeteria.

As I walked through the automatic doors, a blast of heat from above showered me with warmth. If only I could've stayed in its comforting arms forever, but I had to see Dexter before Amber, his girlfriend, or his friends joined him. He went to the cafeteria every morning after swimming training for his breakfast, and he was usually on his own until the others got in.

I turned the corner into the cafeteria. My heart thumped in my chest as I caught sight of him sitting alone in the corner, a Coke bottle in one hand, his iPhone in the other. I'd had a thing about him for, what seemed like, forever. We'd gone to the same primary school but it wasn't until my first year at Riverside that my stomach seemed to go weird and flutter whenever I was around him.

I clasped the earring in my hand even tighter, feeling its edges cutting into the skin on my sweaty palm, and took a step forwards, even though my legs felt like jelly.

And then I stopped.

Tom and Kieran, Dexter's best friends, burst out of the toilet, laughing and shoving each other playfully. They went over to the table and slid into the chairs next to Dexter. Kieran flashed the screen of his mobile at him and Dexter smiled. My whole world seemed to light up.

I almost danced on the spot as a battle raged in me, pulling me in two different directions; did I listen to my head and run away, as fast, and as far, as I could? Or did I act on my heart's desire and speak to him? But his friends? Why were they there? They weren't supposed to be there, not yet.

No. I couldn't do it. Talking to him in front of his friends? What was I thinking? The library seemed like an excellent place to run to. I could hide at the back in the section no one ever went in. I spun around and collided with a tall brunette. Amber.

Amber jumped backwards, her arms spreading wide, her hands up in the air, as if she was trying to avoid touching something disgusting, and her face was screwed up, like a Pug. To think, in year 7, we'd actually been friends. That seemed such a long time ago. Another lifetime even.

'Why don't you just look where you're going?'

I froze. A rabbit caught in headlights, knowing that any moment I was going to be crushed under the wheels of a truck. I felt sick, wanting to spew it all over her nice cream jacket.

'I...I...' I couldn't finish the sentence. It clung to my mouth like a bad taste.

'What do you think you're...' Amber's eyes traced the path of my previous gaze. 'Ha!' she guffawed.

My face blazed crimson.

'Were you spying on Dexter?' Amber looked at me, her head cocked to one side. She put her manicured hands on her hips, and smiled.

I hated that look. The pity. It stripped the warmth from my face and robbed me of any shred of dignity I had left. 'No, I-'

'Don't!' commanded Amber, 'Don't even try to lie about what you were doing!'

'I-'

'As if,' she said, biting out each word as if it were poison, 'he would be interested in a freak like you.' She shook her perfectly coiffured head.

I hated her.

I wanted to be her.

Her expensive perfume was strong, making the urge to vomit even stronger. 'I just wanted to give this back to Dexter,' I said, my voice strangled as I held out my hand, allowing Amber to see the diamond stud that had almost become embedded into my skin.

Amber's eyes narrowed. 'And where did you find that?'

'My place-' I said, looking up to see a flash of anger fly across her face.

'Well,' said Amber, grabbing me by the shoulders, 'don't just stand there!'

She dug her long finger nails into my shoulders, forcing me to turn around. 'Go and give it back to him then,' she said, pushing me in Dexter's direction.

I stumbled forward, struggling to hold back the tears. I wasn't going to cry here, not in front of her, and not in front of them. I held the tears down and pretended I was lying dead at the bottom of the river, free of pain and despair.

Like I said, no one was ever going to see me cry.

I was getting good at playing dead.

Dexter's eyes were fixed on me. I looked away, but I could still see the sneering faces of his friends staring back at me, their eyes full of amusement, waiting for me to slip up, to do something stupid.

'She's got something for you,' said Amber, pushing past me, almost knocking me over. Sniggers bounced around the cafeteria.

'Yeah?' he said, in a sceptical tone. He looked away and began to play with the lid of his Coke bottle.

I slowly shuffled forwards and placed the stud on the table. I would not look up, I would not look at him, and I would not cry, even if that's what I wanted to do more than anything.

'Thanks,' he said, not taking his eyes off his Coke. He made no attempt to retrieve the stud.

Tom Baker, the guy sitting next to Dexter, grabbed his Diesel bag off the table and slid out. 'Love to stay and watch the show but I need to pee. See you guys later,' he said.

Amber slid elegantly into the freshly vacated chair, her hand glancing across Dexter's shoulder. 'She said she found it at her place,' she said, in an almost accusatory tone, but I couldn't quite tell if that was for my benefit, or Dexter's.

Dexter took hold of his bottle and pushed his chair back. He grabbed his bag off the floor and stood up. 'Got to see Mr Charles,' he said to Amber, 'see you English.' Kieran stood up with him.

'Don't forget your stud,' said Amber, holding the sparkling gem up to him, 'although you'll need to give it a good clean before you wear it again.'

'It's okay,' replied Dexter, 'throw it, I've got a million other pairs.' He turned and strode off with Kieran.

Amber stayed seated, and placed the earring in the middle of the table.

'Sit down!' she commanded, as I turned to leave.

I slumped into the chair opposite her, and looked at my hands cupped in front of me.

'Don't think,' said Amber, spitting out the words, 'that just because he took you home, he actually cares about you. He doesn't. You're a freak. No one cares about you, so next time you want to get pissed and fall in the river make sure you never come back out, okay?' She pushed the diamond stud towards me, ' You may as well keep that now you've contaminated it with freakiness. Besides, it's the closest you're ever going to get to him.' Amber's phone began to ring. She slipped her hand into her jacket and pulled out her phone. 'Hi-ya!' she sang into it, 'How're you doing?' Amber rose from her chair and swept out of the cafeteria, not even looking back once.

I remained seated, listening to the quiet after the storm, the sound of a distant hoover, the discordant clattering of pots and pans in the kitchen. My eyes were fixed on the diamond earring in front of me. Its beauty mocked me, its coldness, like ice, spoke to me. I felt so small, like I was the earring lying alone on the table with so much air floating around me. A lone satellite floating in space, feeling nothing but the turning of time, drowning in the emptiness.

An eternity of emptiness. Rolling out like a never-ending ocean.

'Hey, what's up?'

'Sam? What?'

'Are you okay?' Sam's face was tilted, his heavily lined eyes narrowed with concern. 'Heavy Christmas?'

'Yeah, yeah,' I said, brushing the earring onto the floor like a bit of dust, 'I'm fine. Just a bit flat now, need another holiday!' I smiled weakly. So weak that I wasn't convincing anyone, least of all myself.

'What did Amber want?' asked Sam, my best friend. He slid into the chair opposite, plonking his art folder on the table, his fabulous charcoal sketches for our Manga coursework showing through the shiny plastic.

'Oh, nothing. Wow, they're brilliant!' I said, trying to sound as enthusiastic as possible whilst steering the conversation away from what had just happened.

'Thanks. Let's see yours.'

'Shit!' I replied, hitting my head hard with the heel of my hand.

'You've forgotten?'

'No, not exactly,' I replied clasping my hands in front of me. There hadn't seemed much point when I was going to throw myself off the bridge.

'But we've had weeks-'

'I forgot,' I said, shrugging.

Sam clucked. 'I wouldn't like to be in your shoes when we get to class. Miss Powell is going to eat you alive.'

'Well, I'm sure she'll soon spit me back out again. I think my piercings will give her indigestion.'

Sam laughed and shook his head as the bell for Registration rang out. 'You coming?' he said, grabbing his folder and sliding himself out from under the table.

'I'll be there in a minute. Need the toilet first.'

'Okay, see you in a mo.' And with a couple of strides Sam had disappeared around the corner. My beautiful, dependable Sam.

I grabbed my bag off the floor, slid out from under the table, and made my way to the washroom. I threw my bag onto the worktop and looked at myself in the mirror.

I didn't recognise the person staring back at me anymore. Who was I? Where had the girl that I had once known, gone?

Looking at my reflection was like when you lie on your arm in the night and it stops the blood flow, so, when you wake up, your arm is still there but doesn't feel like it's yours.

I pulled out my make-up bag and rummaged through it until I found my favourite Archangel-Red lip gloss. I opened the bottle and rubbed the applicator over my lips. The colour was vibrant, like blood when it first oozes from a fresh wound. Words formed in my head, a poem made like magic. I grabbed my moleskin notebook out of my bag - a birthday present to myself - and began to write:

Knife.
Cold, sharp.
Running across skin,
Makes me feel alive.
Red.

I shoved the notebook and make-up back into my bag and made my way to Registration.

When I eventually got there, the rest of the class were already filing out, their faces sullen and grey as the reality of cold January mornings and A-levels bit deep.

Mr Kirkwood looked up from his computer, and over his thick black glasses perched at the end of his nose. 'You okay now?' he asked, his eyebrows knitted together.

'Er?'

'Sam said you were feeling sick.'

'Oh, yeah. I'm fine. Just feeling a bit rough after Christmas.'

'Not too much partying I hope?'

I smiled weakly.

'Well, if it gets worse just go and see the nurse. We need you fit.'

I nodded back.

'Go on then, off you go to your first class before you get a late mark,' said Mr Kirkwood shooing me out of the room as though I were a fly.

I was the last to arrive in English so I slunk to the back of the room and sat at a spare table at the back, under the great arch window. Mrs Jones stumbled in, hidden under a tower of paper and books. 'Okay. Good morning class,' she said, letting everything tumble out from her arms and onto the table, 'we're going to be looking at the stories of Angela Carter this term. If you'd like to pass the books around.' She grabbed small piles of the books and began feeding them around the class.

'Today we're going to read Bloody Chambers, the first story of the collection, before we do an initial discussion on gender roles, sexuality and the objectification of women in preparation for a presentation, due the first Monday back after half-term. For that, I thought it would be a good idea to put you in mixed pairs-'

A collective groan rumbled around the classroom.

'Okay, okay, settle down,' said Mrs Jones, fanning her hands in the air. 'Mike, sit by Suzy, Taylor by Sarah, Sam by Grace, Dexter, you can go over to Evelyn-'

What?! I looked up, my heart stilled for a moment. I couldn't breathe.

'Evelyn?' asked Dexter, his voice sulky and defiant.

'That's what I said Mr Sullivan,' said Mrs Jones, one hand firmly on her hip, the other pointing at the seat next to me. I felt the warmth of humiliation as it crawled up my neck and onto my face. I stared at her finger still pointing at the chair next to me.

I tuned out, deafened by the blood rushing to my head, a strange mixture of horror and delight pulsing through me as Dexter flopped into the chair and tossed his bag noisily onto the table.

My heart rolled over in my chest. My mouth had dried up like a pool of water in the Sahara. I realised I was kneading my sweaty hands together under the table. How the hell was I supposed to work with him? I Couldn't even speak to him properly. I fixed my eyes on the table in front of me, too afraid to look up in case I looked at him, or, even worse, Amber.

Without even searching her out, I knew she was looking, I felt her blazing fury scorching my skin.

Dexter snatched the book up from the table and opened it to the first page, his body leaning as far away from me as possible.

Was I really that bad?

I cast a furtive glance out of the corner of my eye; his hate for me was written all over his face like the words in a text book. Not that I couldn't blame him. I hated myself more.

But why had he saved me then? Why wasn't I rotting at the bottom of the river?

I took my book off the table, opened it and began to read the first sentence.

And then I read it again.

And again.

But the words didn't make any sense. My head was pounding, my heart quivering in my chest as it struggled to beat.

An image of the Old Bridge flashed before my eyes, I couldn't get it out of my head, it was so clean and crisp, the dank smell of the water so real that I could've been there. And then the feeling of freedom as I plunged into the dark forgiving water.

He should have left me there. He should have let me die.

What a beautiful lie I had believed in.

I stood up, the chair scraping across the wooden floor as I pushed it back. 'I don't feel very well,' I said, my eyes struggling to focus, my heart banging in my chest. Panic was taking flight inside me and I didn't know if I had the strength to fight it. I didn't want to have a crazy, stupid meltdown there.

'What's a matter?' asked Mrs Jones, looking out from under a pile of paperwork.

'I think I'm going to be-'But I didn't finish. I grabbed my book, stuffed it into my bag and ran out of class.

I fled down the stairs and out of the school before anyone had the chance to stop me. All I could picture was the edge of the bridge. The demonic beast wanted to drag me back down into the water. I had to lock the beast down, like Chronos in Tartarus, I had to chain it up, not let it escape until I got home.

In case I did something stupid again.

I didn't stop running until I was safely in the Town Centre, just one girl in a sea of people that no one would take any notice of. Like an automaton, I boarded the number three bus, trying to hold onto the desperation welling up inside of me.

The driver glared at me as I showed him my pass. 'It's the wrong way up love!' he growled.

'The pass,' he barked again, shaking his head and pointing.

I ignored him and headed down the bus, the other passengers clucking and shaking their heads, their faces glaring up at me, twisted and grotesque like demons. But they were staring at me like I was the one with horns sticking out of my head or something. They whispered and laughed. *Why didn't you do it properly? Why are you still here? Waste of space!*

I grabbed on to one of the poles at the side of the aisle to steady myself, and then slowly pulled myself along the bus until I found a spare seat at the back, on my own.

I unzipped my hoodie and tugged at my tee-shirt, trying to allow air in, but I still couldn't breathe. I reached up and opened the window as waves of nausea swept over me. The panic was rising up again, like a cobra, threatening to strike and paralyse me.

'Will you shut that window!' barked a short blonde woman, reaching over me to slam the window shut.

I vaguely heard a male voice say 'These youngsters,' to a chorus of approval, before everything went quiet, and my mind floated off into the distance like I was in a dream, except I knew I wasn't in a dream because I didn't dream.

You had to sleep to dream.

If I could dream, then I would be normal, I could return to life.

Instead, I went back to playing dead.

I let my face fall against the cold wet glass. Outside, the world raced by, distorted by the condensation. I pulled my sleeve over my hand and rubbed the glass, making a small window of clarity.

Tears began to fall.

And there was no stopping them.

Everything was a mess.

Pain shot through my chest, a great physical ache of sadness, like a dagger plunging into me. But instead of killing me, it brought me back to life. I was feeling again and it ached so bad. I wrapped my arms around my chest, trying to hold on to the pain. To stop it spilling out of me with my guts.

No one came to me. No one put their arms around me. They didn't *see* me.

Evie

    I sat on the floor of the shower cubicle, my arms wrapped tightly around my legs, as the scalding water pounded around me. I wore pain like a coat, a second layer of skin. I let the water blast it away, watched it spiral down the plug hole with the water and soap until I could see it no more, until the water had anaesthetised my soul.

    I didn't want to feel anymore.

    I wanted it all to go away.

    Eventually I stumbled out of the cubicle, pulled on my pyjamas and went downstairs. I pulled the convector heater into the conservatory and settled down to draw, curled up on the sofa under a woollen blanket. Outside, night was falling fast, bringing with it an elegant flurry of snowflakes that coated everything in a thin blanket of pure white. As the snow gathered on the roof of the conservatory it felt like I was snuggled in a cocoon of silk, like a caterpillar waiting to transform into a butterfly.

    The pencil lines flowed over the paper, giving me something else to think about as I defined some lines whilst taking the clarity away from others, my hand working almost constantly. I worked late into the evening, the snow still falling from the blanketed sky, until the heater could no longer mask the biting cold and my hands could work no more.

I had my finished sketch for art; a kick-ass warrior girl called Sabre.

My stomach groaned with hunger. I hadn't eaten all day; it just hadn't occurred to me to eat. My Gran, if she'd still been around, would've been appalled. Evelyn, she'd have said, you need to put the calories in to get the energy out. If you don't, you'll get ill.

My Gran. Gone.

How I longed for her to put her arms around me again.

I headed for the kitchen, found a frozen pizza, heated in the microwave then slumped in front of the telly to watch Neighbours and then Home and Away, a whole hour of sunshine television, the kind that you didn't really have to concentrate on, the perfect antidote to cold January days and pizza that tasted of cardboard.

I'd just finished when the doorbell rang. I hoped it wasn't Celia. But it had to be, no one else ever came around, and she only came out of respect for Cassie. Celia hated me, but at least she was honest about it. I respected her for that at least. I fastened my dressing gown and then went and opened the front door.

'Sam? What are you doing here?'

'Hiya!' said Sam, his blues eyes sparkling even in the dark, just like him, 'Just thought I'd come and see if you were alright.'

Sam was always too happy, always too nice, and I didn't deserve him, or his pity. 'Oh, yeah, feeling much better thanks. Must have been something dodgy I ate last night,' I said, rubbing my hand over my stomach, over-emphasising the point.

'Good,' he said, his face tilted slightly. I watched his eyes narrow into slits. I knew he was trying to determine whether I was telling the truth or not, and I wasn't going to help him out on that.

There was an awkward pause before he continued, 'It was probably a good job you didn't go to art today, Miss Powell was in a right foul mood,' he said, blowing a snowflake off his nose, 'one of the year nines had super-glued the acrylic pots to the worktops. She couldn't get them off, had to get the Caretaker to do it.'

'Oh,' I said, searching around for something to say, finally settling on, 'Anyone we know?'

'Graham Higgins,' said Sam, stamping his feet in the thickening snow, his breath escaping in wisps from his mouth.

'Oh,' I repeated.

Sam's gaze dropped to the floor. 'I was wondering whether you wanted help with your art coursework, you know, as you'd forgotten it. Thought you might not have done it? You didn't really say earlier...' He left the question dangling in the air.

Paranoia kicked me in the guts. Why was he asking me this now? Did he know about my run-in with the river? No, he didn't know, did he? Whatever, I had no intention of answering his question. 'Look Sam, now's really not a good time, I'd invite you in, but mom's just about to put tea out.' I said, gesturing behind me with a quick flick of my head.

'Oh.' he said, with a weak smile that would usually have me crippled with guilt, 'oh okay then, just thought...you know. Anyway, I'll see you tomorrow?'

'Yeah, I'll see you tomorrow.'

'Ok. Bye,' said Sam, raising his hand to wave goodbye and then thinking better of it.

I closed the door on him before he'd even left the driveway.

My home was my sanctuary and I didn't want anyone coming in and spoiling that. Not even my best friend. Especially not my best friend. I couldn't let him in, couldn't let anyone see how far I'd fallen. I didn't want to be his burden. I didn't want his pity, or his love, I didn't deserve it. I wanted to be alone in the only place I that I could truly be myself.

And yet, when I went back into the living room, the quiet crashed over me, dead and silent like a graveyard and I hated it. I hated the feeling of nothingness, the complete emptiness that opened up like a vast ocean in front of me. I was floating in the middle of it, keeping my head barely above the surface, miles and miles of black sea stretching out from me in every direction.

I didn't want to be with people. I didn't want to be alone. My conundrum. A complete contradiction that made me feel that I didn't belong anywhere, especially in this world.

That's why I'd tried to end it. I just wanted it all to stop. There was no other way out.

I went to bed to avoid the silence, the emptiness of the house. Maybe today I would be able to fall to sleep and then, for a few blissful hours, I wouldn't be able to feel or think.

I climbed in to bed and wrapped myself up in my plump patchwork quilt that smelt of summer and bright flowers and happiness, but inside me the ball of dread was beginning to roll in my stomach. How long would it be before I finally fell to sleep? Sometimes it could be hours, and on a few occasions I'd fallen to sleep just as my morning alarm shrieked. I would lie, still and silent like I was dead, watching the shadows dance across the room, hours and hours swallowed whole by the long expanse of silence and darkness.

I shut my eyes and grotesque images danced across the back of my eyelids, laughing at me from the corners of my mind. I opened my eyes, tried to avoid them by staring at the ceiling, but the shadows began to laugh at me too as they started to creep across, dripping down the sides of the walls like big black spider webs. The monsters of my mind began to take form in the shadows, encouraged by the demonic beast; the Raven of the Edgar Allan Poe poem, who came gently rapping, rapping...Deep into that darkness peering...dreaming dreams no mortal ever dared to dream before.

I had become so fearful of my own mind, of my deepest darkest thoughts. Sometimes, in the past, in the depths of the night, after finally falling to sleep, I'd wake up, not knowing what was real or what was a dream, the two worlds had somehow started to collide and merge into one.

The dreams where I'd slashed my wrists were the worst; I'd wake up drenched in sweat, not able to tell if I was alive or dead.

And then even the dreams stopped visiting.

The lines of the poem ran through my mind until the Sandman eventually took me into his arms.

Evie

When I woke early the next day, I bounded out of bed and flung open the curtains; outside was blanketed in a thick carpet of snow. There was no way on this earth that Mr Taylor would open the school - he lived too far away- and for one more day at least, I wouldn't have to deal with anyone - no Sam, no Amber, no teachers and definitely no Dexter. I couldn't deal with that. I didn't want the beast getting any help in plunging and twisting the knife into my gut.

I grabbed my laptop and went downstairs. It was coffee that I needed more than anything.

I dropped my laptop on the dining table and went into the kitchen, made coffee and let the invigorating aroma wake me up. I took it into the dining room and fired up the laptop.

I signed into my e-mail account first; it'd been a while since I'd heard off Cassie, not that that was unusual. When it came to Cassie, I seemed to be right at the bottom of her list of priorities. I wondered how long it would've taken her to find out I was dead, if I had succeeded in killing myself. Would she have cut short her holiday? Probably not.

She was due back on the Fourteenth, in six days, but, to be honest, with Cassie, no one actually knew until she was stood there in front of you.

I flicked my eyes over the list of e-mails, ignoring most of them - especially those from Ali57, Razorgirl and other names I recognised but not because they were friends - and scrolled down to Cassiealex, double-clicking on it to open it.

7th January 7.09 pm

Hi Hun,

Me and Dan are having such a good time that we've decided to stay on a little longer, maybe an extra week? Have a feeling he's going to propose to me!!! Wish me luck.

Mom xx

I looked up, feeling the ghost of her presence in the room, from the expensive candles, to the oversized cushions on the sofa, and the picture of us both on the mantelpiece, taken in happier times, when my father was still alive. I think I was five or six, and it was my birthday. We'd been shopping for my first Barbie (it was the most beautiful doll I had ever seen, with a pure white gown and feathers in her hair. I still have her somewhere, locked up with other memories that are too painful to think about). My father had taken us to McDonalds for dinner. I remember when we sat down to eat, he made a little silver ring, engraved with the letter "E", magically appear from the back of my ear. I thought it was magic, but now I know differently.

I shivered. For some reason, at that moment, I really missed him.

And I felt her absence in the empty space in the house too, the gaping hole that should've been Cassie.

Cassie. My mother.

I looked back at the message on the computer screen. I stared at the words, let them sink into my soul.

The demonic beast was stirring again; he was really hungry and he gobbled up the words of her message with relish. I flopped back in my chair and massaged the knot in my right shoulder.

Cassie was getting engaged.

Again.

To another no hoper.

Cassie had been engaged three times since my father had died. And then there were the ones in between, the randoms, whose names and faces I didn't know and Cassie herself probably couldn't even remember. Her relationships were a kind of sick ritual, a cycle of self-harm where Cassie fell for the wrong guy, ended up hurt and humiliated, drank herself silly, then after a few weeks, hooked up with someone else.

Simon was the first I could remember. I hated him, and not just because he was the first guy Cassie had dated after my father had died, although that would've been bad enough on its own. Simon was a complete creep who used to spend most days drinking and smoking pot. He lasted about six months before Cassie found him in bed with his best mate.

The second was Dave, a complete slob who just leered at anything female with a pulse, including me. I remember the hungry look he used to give me with his bloodshot eyes. The thought of him still made my skin crawl. I couldn't remember why Cassie had split up with him - and I didn't want to think about it too much - but I was very glad when it fizzled out, despite the months of

Cassie's mad antics after it. I remember leaving the house for school on a Monday morning, when I was about eleven or twelve, and finding her curled up outside on the doorstep, drunk.

The third guy was over so quick that I didn't even know his name. In fact, I didn't even meet him, just the devastation after he'd passed through. I nicknamed him Hurricane.

And now there was Dan.

He and Cassie had been together for about seven months and they were "in love". He was a nice enough bloke, I suppose, but still, past experience told me it was only a matter of time.

I slouched forward in my chair, crossing my legs underneath it, and took a good swig of coffee as I clicked on the e-mail from Razorgirl. I knew what was coming, but for some reason looking at these vile e-mails had somehow become my own sick ritual, poking the knife in my never-to-heal wound.

But this time it was different. An image of my own face flashed upon the screen. My eyes were shut like I was sleeping, my ghost-like face splattered with mud.

I sat frozen, strangely entranced by the grotesque image on the screen. I couldn't ever remember a time when I had looked so peaceful, so beautiful. And yet looking at my own dead face terrified me. Someone had taken a photo of me when I was...

I felt sick. Dexter had saved me, brought me home, but who had taken this photo? Who had seen me first?

I stared at the photo, something was pulling inside me, making me look. Underneath the image were the words "Next time, do it properly. BITCH!"

I clicked on delete and the next e-mail flashed up on my screen. It contained the same picture, this time with only two words; "Just die!"

I slammed the top of my laptop down and swept the mug of coffee off the table with my hand. Coffee splashed up the wall and the mug crashed to the floor, smashing into lots of tiny pieces. Like my life.

Even after I'd closed the computer down, the image still burned in my mind, like someone had branded it onto my vision with a red hot poker. There was a war raging inside me and I wasn't winning.

I leapt up, letting the chair fall to the floor with a crash, and fled upstairs.

Yanking my clothes off, I flung them on the bathroom floor and stumbled into the shower.

The scalding water felt good against my freezing cold skin. I - again - imagined it washing the pain and the anger away and watched as it all was sucked down the plughole with the soap. It was purifying me, allowing me to wrestle back control.

When I felt like I had been washed clean, I stepped out of the shower and grabbed the towel to dry myself. I stopped stone dead as I caught sight of my reflection in the mirror; I was grotesque and miss-formed with bits of bone jutting out here and there. How had I got so thin? Food had become boring and dull and didn't seem worth the effort. Eating had become more of a chore than a pleasure and, as everyone knows, chores were there to be avoided.

I got dressed and flopped on to my bed, my hair still dripping wet, and I stared up at the ceiling; I was supposed to be distracting myself, not pulling myself deeper into thinking about things. About me, the chaos that was my life.

I needed more coffee, so I went back downstairs. The coffee I'd thrown had marked the wall in the dining room. It had dried on like a congealed blood stain in a crime scene. I knew that no matter how much I scrubbed at the stain, the smell would mark my flesh like the blood-stained hands of Lady Macbeth.

And there, on the table, was the laptop. I could almost hear it whispering to me, tempting me to look at those ghostly images, like the Sirens calling sailors to their death on the jagged rocks. The voices told me to look. They told me to open up the wounds again, that picking at them with a sharp knife would make me feel better.

Now that I felt pain again, I had started to crave it like a drug; it made me feel alive, made me feel wanted and yet, when I was in pain, I longed to push it away and feel nothing again. To play dead. Another conundrum, another reason why I didn't belong in this world.

Not even fighting it, I opened one of the e-mails and the image flashed up. My image, although it felt as though it was someone else lying there, cold and blue. It didn't feel like it had happened to me, and only a few days ago. My ghostly-white face looked like it was carved from marble, an angel encircled by a halo of darkness, as if all my impurities, my sins, had leeched from my skin. But they were only petrol black feathers of a crow.

Only in death could I be truly beautiful.

Something flickered inside me, an image, a forgotten memory. It danced across my vision and then was gone, but its echo remained, telling me that it had once lived outside of my mind.

The feathers.

I had seen one in my room, the day after my "accident".

I raced upstairs and flung open my bedroom door. The room was a tip, and still smelt rancid even though I'd changed the bed covers.

When had I started living like this? I disgusted myself. I hated living in mess, but it was like some switch that went off in my head when Cassie was away, a silent way of sticking two fingers up to her. It was always the same; she came home, saw my room, we'd have a slanging match and then Cassie would storm off and go to Celia's. Again.

I began to rummage through the junk on my floor; old essays, sketches, dirty clothes (including socks that would probably stick to the wall), lipstick stained tee-shirts, CDs, DVDs, (and their empty covers) lined the floor like a second carpet. I flung everything on the bed, but even when it was piled high, only the dirty carpet left on the floor, I didn't find a single feather, even though I knew it had to be there, I could feel it.

And then I remembered the day Celia came around; I had seen that feather on the top of my stinking clothes. I plummeted down the stairs and into the utility room where I'd left the washing I'd done over the last few days. I'm not even going to pretend I'm good at laundry; most days I take clothes off and file them on my floor, then, the next day if they smell okay, they're clean enough for me. I grabbed the clothes basket and tipped the contents out. There, snuggled in amongst the clean laundry, was a single black feather, all tattered and bent.

It was one of the most beautiful feathers I have ever seen, even though it was damaged. The main shaft, the rachis, was probably thirty centimetres long, with beautifully soft, but equally strong, barbs that looked black at a distance but on close inspection where actually made up from all the colours of the rainbow, like petrol on a wet floor. I locked it in my wooden box on my dressing table; the place that I kept all of my most precious things, before I turned my attention to finally cleaning my bedroom.

Josh

I hated the frailness of my new status; half human, half angel. A freak. The weakness I carried around with me was like a disease, sapping my strength, making my new-born wings heavy, my body tired.

I flew over the Atlantic ocean, accompanied only by the stars and the sound of the wind and the waves, arriving in Harlem deep in the dead of the night.

I stood in front of the Brownstone house, snowflakes flittering around me on the squally breeze like faeries, their wings illuminated by the golden glow of the street lamps. Snow lay in piles at the edge of the frozen pavement; a white wall that extended in both directions for as far as I could see.

The townhouse looked derelict, with its flaking paint and boarded-up windows covered in flyers for local gigs and bars, but I knew an angel lived there; I could hear the muffled notes of the angel's celestial music coming from behind its crumbling facade.

I stood beneath one of the leafless trees that lined the avenue and listened, deciphering as best as I could, the sorrowful, simple notes that repeated over and over again.

This angel was a Watcher, and had been for a very, very long time.

A clock struck three.

I carefully climbed the ice covered steps up to the front door, its crumbling archivolt covered in green moss and dirt. I rapped my knuckles on it three times, then waited.

There was a thump, and a brief pause, before the door slowly creaked open, angelic music sweeping out of the house through the widening crack in the doorway; lamenting fingers of celestial harmony which wrapped themselves around me, massaging my aching bones and filling me with an inner warmth.

An elderly angel stood bent double in the doorway, his slender frame hidden beneath multi-coloured layers of frayed cardigans, all tied around his waist with a belt of knotted string, his umber wings, flecked with tawny gold, protruded from slits cut in the back. Despite his age and frailness, this angel was beautiful; his weathered face, although etched with wrinkles that told of centuries of life spent in the human world, was alive with warmth, compassion and beauty.

'Hell-' The angel stopped, his eyes, although covered in a white layer of cataracts, bore into me, with a look so intense it made my skin prickle. 'You're an Angel of Death?'

'I am-'

'So, it is time,' he said gently, bowing his head.

'No! No. I mean, I was an Angel of Death, but that's not why I'm here,' I said, hastily backing away from the door.

'Oh, I-' The old angel swayed on the spot, throwing his hand out to steady himself on the doorway, but he missed and started to fall towards the floor as his legs buckled under him.

I raced forward, catching him before he hit the ground. Shockwaves of raw pain crashed through me with the memories of the angel's life on earth, each layer of the man's existence pushing itself into my mind, forcing me down onto my knees under the burden of it.

I couldn't fight it, it was too powerful, so I surrendered.

In my mind, I entered his life.

I found myself standing in a field of lush green crops, the sun burning high above in the azure sky. Around me, people were digging, weeding or carrying harvested crops in large wicker baskets hoisted upon their heads - all gravitating around the vast white marble mansion that stood in the centre of the fields, like the planets around the sun - singing in unison, a lament of beauty that told of misery and longing.

But, despite the heat and the burning of the sun in the sky, a brutal darkness lurked amongst the cotton plants, a sinister feeling that clawed deep into my skin.

'Obadiah!'

I turned to see where the voice had come from. A woman stared back at me, her eyes the colour of golden amber, and when she smiled my heart felt like it would break. I tried to speak but the words caught in the back of my throat with my breath.

Love coursed through my body like blood.

She folded her fingers through mine, her other hand resting on her round, protruding stomach and for the briefest of moments, I felt totally at peace.

And then she was gone.

I turned around to look for her, but darkness was falling fast, clouding my vision. In the sky, dark, threatening clouds smothered the blood red moon and a cold wind whipped up around me, throwing up grit that bit into my flesh.

On the horizon I could just make out figures, cloaked in white, dancing around blazing fires of gold. A bloodcurdling scream was cut short by thunder as it rumbled around the sky. A flash of lightning ripped the dark apart, illuminating a woman's body hanging lifeless from the branches of a poplar tree, the flames of fury licking at her feet.

All of this had happened in the past. This horror was a fragment of Obadiah's memory unfolding before me and inside of me. I stood there, unable to save his soul-mate but also unable to look away. I felt his pain, felt his heart being torn from his chest like it was my own.

Like waking from a nightmare, it took a few moments for my mind to clear, to tell what was real and what was not; I was lying on my side in the doorway of the house, entangled in Obadiah's body.

I untangled myself from him and stood up. The room was freezing, filled with light flurries of snow from the open doorway, so I dragged him inside, then closed the door, shutting out the artic wind and snow.

The house smelt like old books, mouldy paper and coffee. I looked over to the large oak table. Every inch of its surface was covered in books, vellums or chunky candles with tears of hardened wax spilling down their sides. A half-drunk mug of coffee sat next to a warm carafe and an opened book.

I grabbed the carafe, refilled the mug, and took it to Obadiah, lifting his head up, to let the warm coffee moisten his lips, and waited for the aroma to revive him.

His eyes flickered open and he pushed the mug away with his trembling hand. 'I'm sorry...I don't know....what-'

'It's okay,' I said, as he tried to lift himself up off the ground. I put the mug on the floor and grabbed onto his arms to help him up.

'No, it's not.'

'It was the shock-'

'No, not shock,' he said, 'shock didn't knock Obadiah off his feet.' He shook his head. 'The crashing waves of disappointment knocked me down.' He pointed his crooked finger at the table, telling me, I think, that he wanted to sit down.

I pulled the angel to his feet and led him to the table.

He nodded his head in thanks and slumped into the chair. 'I need coffee, and plenty of it.'

I grabbed his mug, refilled it and offered it to him. He took it with both hands and gulped it down. He dropped the mug on the table and wiped the corner of his mouth with the sleeve of his cardigan, before grabbing the carafe and pouring himself another cup. 'I've been waiting for so long, and after I told Her about Hyperion, I thought She might finally let me go. Then you show up, an Angel of Death...I thought...you...and then...' He sighed, and let his head fall forward in defeat. 'How long must I wait?' he said, gently to himself.

I slipped into the chair opposite him. 'You want to die?'

He looked at me, the despair clearly written in the lines on his face. He nodded. 'Obadiah is tired, so very tired. But She won't let me go.

It struck me, in the silence of that room, that we both had what the other wanted. He had life, I had death.

Finally, he spoke again. 'I just thought.' He closed his eyes and rested his forehead in the palm of his hand. 'I'm sorry, for my mistake,' he said, opening his eyes. 'You must forgive an old angel's blindness, in my haste I missed the disruption in your aura, the slight distortion of your music. It's as if parts of you are missing or something is interfering with it, like some of your powers have been taken away?'

'Yes, but how can you-'

'See?' Obadiah smiled, and for a moment his face came alive. 'This is confusing you?' he said, pointing to his milky white eyes, 'Obadiah is almost blind to the world, but can still see many, many things.' He reached his hand out across the table, 'The name's Obadiah, pleased to meet you.'

I took his hand in mine, let the pain, his pain, the memories, soak deep within me. 'Josh, I'm Josh.'

'Sorry,' said Obadiah, wrenching his hand away, 'I see that your gift, of taking the pain of others away, ain't one of them powers you've lost?'

I nodded.

Obadiah bowed his head. 'I will make sure I ain't touching you then.'

'What is this place?' I asked, looking at the bookshelves covering every available wall in the house, each overflowing with leather bound books, rolled up parchments, vellums and modern paperbacks, written in every language you could possibly think of.

'It's the place I call home,' he said. He took a sip of coffee before continuing. 'So, if you're not here to take Obadiah, you must be here because She sent you to ask me about Hyperion?'

'Yes, She wants me to find him. The Virtues are having trouble locating him, there's something wrong with their instruments.' I watched Obadiah's white eyebrows knit together. 'She said that the last place he visited, for certain, was here?'

'Yes,' said Obadiah, nodding his head vigorously, ' I didn't know who he was when he arrived, his angelic music was weak and deformed, and easily disguised by the storm he rode in on.'

'Weak and deformed? Like my music?'

'No,' said Obadiah, 'your music is distorted, but it's still the music of an angel. It may have been interfered with but you can still see your history, your fingerprint hidden within them notes. Beneath the distortion it's still your signature tune, the melody of Josh, an Angel of Death. Hyperion's music was almost unrecognisable as the mark of an angel, let alone that of an Archangel. It was damaged, like it had been blackened by fire.'

'How can it be damaged?'

'I don't know for sure,' he said, stroking the tight white curls on his head, 'but it was only because he told me, that I knew who he was. That an Archangel's music could change so much, that he could speak with such a fervent madness.' He sighed loudly, before continuing, 'It un-nerved me, put me on edge. I could feel the madness burning inside him, on the verge of spilling out.'

'And so you told Death?'

'No,' he said, gently shaking his head. Obadiah grabbed the mug off the table and took another sip of coffee. He lowered it, resting his hand on his stomach. 'I reported him because of them things he spoke of.'

I looked at Obadiah, at his heavy brow, the lines of worry trailing across his face. 'And what did he speak of?' I asked, my body automatically leaning towards him as the presence of evil made itself felt in the air.

'He asked Obadiah if he knew of the ritual of Cleaving,' he replied, his voice lowered to a whisper.

'Cleaving?' I said, shaking my head, 'I don't know what that is.'

'I would've been worried if you did,' he said, placing his mug down on the table. He reached into his trouser pocket and fetched out a small silver flask. 'Them ain't natural things to be talking about, that's why I told Her.' He unscrewed the top of the flask, took a small sip of its contents before offering it to me.

'No, thanks,' I said, 'So what is Cleaving?'

He tipped the rest of the flask into his mug. 'An Angel's soul has two parts, the Divine Spark of Life and -'

'The Arkhe.'

'That's right. The Arkhe is the part of an angel's soul where our music comes from, whereas the Divine Spark is the seat of our immortality, the place that animates us. Together they make an angel's essence, there ain't one without the other.

'A long time ago, before the One-hundred-thousand-year Truce, them Demons used to trap us and extract our Divine Spark, so that they could eat it. Cleaving was the name given to the process of extracting it.'

'They used to extract it, and eat it?' Suddenly I felt sick.

'Oh yes,' said Obadiah, 'Them demons loved to devour our Divine Spark, gives them a high and all sorts of crazy stuff.' He discarded the empty flask on the table, 'But they won't touch the Arkhe, you see it's deadly poisonous to them, turns them to stone from the inside out.'

'But why would Hyperion want-'

'Patience. I'm getting to it,' he said, holding his hand up to quieten me. 'The Divine Spark has to be taken whilst the angel still lives, else it's no good, it dies when the angel dies and loses all its potency. But them wily demons worked out a way to keep the angel alive just long enough to extract the living Spark-'

'How?'

'They have an elixir to keeps the angel alive, but in a state of catatonia, whilst extraction takes place.'

'Sounds like torture.'

'It's the worst kind of torture. You would not believe.'

'So Hyperion wants to torture other angels?'

Obadiah shook his head. 'No, though that would be bad enough. No, our brother, Hyperion, wanted to know if there was any way to alter the process, to use Cleaving on himself to cleave his Arkhe from his own soul, leaving his Divine Spark behind, and that's truly the horror of it.'

'But why would he want to cleave his own Arkhe? Why would you do that?'

'I don't know. Even with all my years as an angel, I ain't never come across such a thing. This is a dangerous, un-natural thing Hyperion wants to do. That's what I told him and that's why I told Her.'

'Would it kill him?'

'No one knows, not even them demons, but let me say this,' said Obadiah, pointing his crooked finger at me, 'even if he could do it, and remain alive, well, he would never be the same again, he would be damaged, broken in ways we can't even imagine.'

'Why did he come here? Why did he come to you?'

Obadiah shrugged. 'He thought I had the answers he needed.'

'And?'

'I may be a Watcher, I may have access to certain information, but Obadiah don't deal with them kind of evil things.'

'So what happened next, when you told him you didn't have the answers?'

Obadiah lifted his mug to his lips and took a sip. I noticed his hand was badly shaking. He placed the mug back on the table to hide the tremor. 'I ain't gonna discuss them things. I sent him away, told him, if you really want to know them things you need to find a copy of the Necrodemonicon-'

'The what?'

'The Necrodemonicon. It's a most evil book, written by them demons. If he wants to find out about them things, that is where he must look, not here,' he said, tapping his chest with his finger. 'I told him to go and find it and leave Obadiah out of it.'

'And where would he find this Necrodemonicon?'

'The place that most of them evil things end up,' he said, 'The Vatican.'

'The Vatican? If this book is as evil and demonic as you say it is, why would it be in the most holy of cities?'

Obadiah's eyebrows knitted together and, despite his blindness, he looked straight at me and shook his head. 'Most holy of cities? I know you don't believe that-'

'No, but it still doesn't make sense-'

'It makes perfect sense,' said Obadiah, relaxing back in his chair, 'the Vatican loves power, information is power, books contain information-'

'Yeah, but still, demonic books?'

'Even demonic books. They collect whatever they can find; texts that support their theories about God, religion, and their more warped ideas,' said Obadiah, waving his hands wildly in the air, 'especially their more warped ideas. Yes, them texts that validate their teachings are paraded about like rum in a Speakeasy. But them demonic texts, them evil things are hidden right beside the books and texts that don't fit in with their ideals and philosophies.'

'How could they hide all those books? Someone must know-'

'Of course, but contact with them is restricted. Only the most trusted, most faithful to the Vatican have access to this Forbidden library.'

'A Forbidden library?'

'Yes. It's hidden in a vast vault located deep in the bowels of the Castel Sant' Angelo, in Rome-'

'Are you sure? How do you know all of this?' I studied his face looking for answers.

'Because I have been there,' he said, 'but only once, a long, long time ago.'

'How long ago did Hyperion leave?'

'Eight moons ago.'

'I should go to Rome, find out what he's up to. He might still be there, if I'm lucky-'

'I doubt he'll be there now, but, it's a place to start,' he said, shrugging. Obadiah reached forward and patted my hand, sending little tremors of pain and sadness pulsing through me. 'Be careful, something tells me brother Hyperion is more than a little crazy and not to be messed with lightly.'

'Thank you,' I said, as I stood up, 'for all your help.'

Obadiah rose to his feet and nodded. 'Can you do me one little favour in return?'

He didn't even need to ask, I knew what he wanted, the pained look on his face told me all I needed to know. 'What?'

'Succeed in whatever it is you're doing and, when you're done, come back for me, sever my life, let Obadiah go to Nancy.'

I put my hand on his shoulder, despite the pain. 'If I could take you, I would. I would take all of your sorrow, wipe it all so you could feel it no more and I would escort you to Nancy, but I'm no longer in possession of those powers. It isn't your time to die.'

'But when you get them powers back, come back for me, set me free?'

'I will,' I said, unable to deny his last request.

Josh

I flew back over the Atlantic ocean, the star encrusted sky vanishing as its mistress, the sun, appeared on the horizon, her alchemical touch transforming its dark waters from black, to indigo, to ultramarine and finally cerulean. On this crossing, for some inexplicable reason, I was drawn to the water like a child with a new toy, gliding down to smell its delicious saltiness, to watch how the sunlight danced upon it, the golden web of light fracturing as dolphins broke the surface, inviting me to play. I revelled in its beauty, basked in the glory of the sun, and delighted in the caress of the wind as it tousled my feathers. I was finally awakening after almost three centuries of being asleep.

But my delight soon faded as exhaustion seeped into my bones, making my wings feel like they were on fire. I grew weaker, tormented by thoughts of Evie. I pictured her, jumping from the bridge, and imagined what would've happened if I hadn't been there to save her.

'And yet, she still might try and take her own life again...' Death's words played with my mind; what if Evie were to do it again? No. I would not let myself think like that.

I pushed on through my fatigue, knowing that every wing beat took me closer to Rome, one step closer to Hyperion and one step closer to my freedom. My misery would soon be over; I'd remind Hyperion of his obligations, then go back to Death and gladly let her take me.

The sun had long since fallen below the horizon when I finally made Rome. The city glistened beneath me, a maze of narrow medieval streets, ancient temples and fountains still bustling with street sellers and tourists. I headed for Saint Peter's, passing over its golden cross, and the Piazza San Pietro that lay beyond, hidden from the brightly coloured Swiss Guards by my loyal friend, Nyx, the night. She kept me cloaked and concealed from prying eyes and would never betray me.

Just beyond Saint Peter's lay the Castel Sant' Angelo, a jewel sparkling from the edge of the river Tiber, the bronze statue of the Archangel Michael illuminated at its apex (Not that the statue was anything like Michael; he's actually short and quite plump, with a bald head and wouldn't be seen dead with a sword).

I lingered by Michael, listening for any trace of Hyperion's music, hoping that he hadn't cleaved yet (I didn't know what I was exactly listening for, but hoped his music was as distinctive as Obadiah had said it was).

I tuned out the noises of the city, but the screams of past horrors coming from the Castel were not so easily ignored; they were too loud, nearly overwhelming my senses. The stories of death, the ghosts that lingered, were all speaking to me, fighting to get their voices heard. I disregarded their pleas and managed to lock on to a harmony - despite the turbulent sea of sound - that was like nothing I had ever heard. It was discordant, like the scratching of a thousand out of tune violins burning in hell, and it was coming from somewhere deep within the Castel. Was this Hyperion's music and was he still in the Forbidden Library?

I landed on a courtyard on the third floor, its cobbled floor littered with piles of cannon balls and medieval weaponry. The tip of my wing brushed the edge of a wooden ballista and revulsion rocked my body, momentarily stealing my vision as images of death, torture and battlefields forced themselves upon me. I let them subside, let them fall from my mind like rain, before turning my attention to gaining access into the Castel.

I pulled the iron grill off a wooden door and shoved it open with my shoulder. I pinned my wings back and stepped over the threshold and into the dark.

Slowly my eyes adjusted to the lack of light. I could see that the room was filled with glass cabinets containing medieval armour and weapons. The cries of the slain told me of their suffering, their memories now embedded in the walls of the Castel like hidden blood stains at a murder scene.

I passed through and quickly located a map of the fortress' interior; I was on the floor that had contained the prison, torture rooms and food stores which were connected to the rest of the Castel by a long corridor that spiralled down to the lowest level plotted on the map. I knew from what Obadiah had said that the Forbidden library was located deep within the bowels of the Castel, and wouldn't be located on any map. I took the corridor down as far as I could before I lifted up a metal grill in the floor and eased myself through the small hole.

I found myself in a tunnel, hewn roughly out of the tufa rock, too narrow for me to unfurl my wings so I let them fade away into nothing but a pile of worthless feathers. The air was warm and stale, smelling of sulphur and stagnating water from the river that coursed nearby.

Down in the bowels of the earth, it was easier to hear Hyperion's music, so I followed its path, letting every subtle shift in pattern or tone direct my way. The terrain was hard to navigate; the floor was uneven, the labyrinthine tunnels were cramped, barely illuminated by what was left of my pathetic angelic glow.

I stopped at the mouth of yet another passage. My way was blocked by a rusty iron gate hanging limply off its hinges. Hyperion's residual harmony was particularly strong at this point, almost as if he had lingered at that point for a while. I tossed the gate aside, knowing I was on the right path, and continued deeper into the guts of the earth, descending into Hell, like Dante in Inferno.

The air was becoming hot and thick with the stench of death - my mistress' aroma - and it made the anger twist even tighter in my stomach. Skeletons grinned at me from beds cut out of the tufa rock, their smiles distorted by decay. Now and again, the walls opened up into little rooms, or cubicula, where the rich, in times past, would lay their deceased loved ones so that they could come and feast with them. But to me, there was only bone there and nothing else; no remaining thread of the soul or life.

The passageway finally opened out into a circular chamber lit by a series of small flickering lights tacked onto the rock wall, with a single exit leading off it. The room itself was plain, except for the intricate mosaic floor depicting the Christian martyrs, Saint Peter the Exorcist and Saint Marcellinus. Their faces were easily recognisable despite the thin layer of dirt on top of them; I had seen them many times in funerary art, but in this chamber they looked out of place, their energy feeling very different, as if the Saints were trying to provide some sort of protection from the feeling of evil that was beginning to filter into the room from the floor below.

I braced myself against the wall and rammed my heel into the tiles. My foot smashed right through leaving a ragged hole through which I could see another circular room beneath me. I stamped on the floor again and again until the hole was big enough for me to fit through, then I carefully lowered myself through the gap into the room below.

This room was much bigger than the one I had just left and more richly decorated. An eight pointed star sparkled on the black marble floor like a compass, each golden point corresponding to a doorway.

I stood in the middle of the star listening for Hyperion. I took the corridor directly in front of me, the harsh strangled notes of violins coming from deep within it told me Hyperion had passed through there recently. The air was thick with the smell of paraffin from the glass lamps hanging on the walls, and unstable. I could sense that something had disturbed the air in the corridor, as the remnants of the disturbance hung over the overflowing shelves of diabolical texts like ghostly cobwebs.

I followed the corridor until I reached the first major intersection; a circular reading room lined in white Carrara marble. Eight large niches had been carved into the walls, each lit with a small lamp and with its own wooden stool and desk. Eight more corridors, spaced equally between the alcoves, led off from this reading room.

Again I tracked Hyperion's musical trail, taking the second exit to the left, down the curving path of books until I reached a spot stained heavily with Hyperion's scent. I scanned the shelves for any clues, tracing my fingers over the spines of the books. They seemed to shudder under my touch as though they were alive, willing me to open them up so that they might, at last, reveal their mysteries again, but they offered none of Hyperion's secrets up to me in return.

The shelves were crammed full of books on things such as identifying Holy bones, Classifying Relics, Rituals for de-sanctifying Reliquaries and The Magic of Ancient Relics. There was no Necrodemonicon, or anything relating to the process of cleaving angelic music.

What was Hyperion up to?

I was suddenly aware of a burning presence to the side of me, a flickering fire out of the corner of my eye. I turned, feeling the adrenaline racing through my body. 'Hyperion?'

'I am, indeed,' said Hyperion, his face ignited by a devilish smile. 'I see my reputation precedes me.'

Hyperion was beautiful, a golden star in the darkness of these catacombs. He was over seven feet tall - much taller than me - with skin the colour of burnished copper and golden eyes that burnt like fire. But despite his beauty, I could see the corruption Obadiah had spoken about, the rot that was beginning to devour him; there was a ring of black that surrounded him at the very innermost part of his aura, singeing parts of his flesh black. On his stomach red swollen wounds weaved across his flesh, interlaced with older scars. His wings, pinned against his back, were flames of gold, that flickered like a candle as he moved towards me.

'I'm assuming She has sent you?' he said, cocking his head to the side.

'If you mean Death-'

'Who else would it be?' he asked. It was only now that I noticed the red leather book he held in his right hand. Was this the Necrodemonicon? 'It is always Death!' he said, drawing my gaze back to his face. I noticed his face burned with an intense anger almost bordering on madness. 'The bitch just won't leave me alone, like a dog on heat. But anyway.' He ran his free hand through the flames of his hair. He took a sharp intake of breath then exhaled loudly, I think, to calm himself. 'What does She want now?' he asked.

'She has sent me to remind you of your obligations-'

'My obligations?' Hyperion cut in, his free hand clutching his chest, 'Well, ain't that just grand? I take a little bit of time off and the whole world falls apart.'

Hyperion moved closer. 'I only came to look a few things up and She gets all histrionic on me. Here, take a look,' he said, holding out the book to me. 'Women, eh?'

I took the book from him, feeling his fingers of fire brush mine. It struck me that, for all the fire, they lacked any warmth.

'Actually,' said Hyperion, crossing his arms over his chest, 'don't. The light here is terrible. Why don't we go back through to the reading room? The light in there is so much better.' He smiled at me, or, at least I think it was a smile, a smile that hinted at things thought but not spoken.

Hyperion gestured for me to walk back the way I had come from. I turned, silently obeying him, but my gut was telling me that danger was not far away. His presence burned behind me as I walked; from the heat on my skin and the burning of the air around me.

I reached the middle of the reading room and turned to face him.

'Go on,' he said, 'take a look. I think you'll find the third chapter very interesting.'

I remained still, ignoring Hyperion's suggestion.

A smirk played upon Hyperion's copper-coloured lips. 'Don't read it then, makes no difference to me,' he said, as he began to circle around me like I was dinner.

I looked straight ahead, ignoring the strong desire to watch him like a hawk. He circled me once, then came to a stop behind me and ran his cold finger nail down my spine. I shuddered as it came to a full stop in the small of my back. I stood up taller as I felt him move in closer, his warm breathe skimming across the skin on my neck, his nail still stabbing at the base of my back.

'It's interesting, don't you think, that She has sent you to remind me of my obligations?' He spoke quietly into my ear.

I fought the impulse to turn around.

'As if you could,' he said, moving around me, dragging his nail across my skin. He came to a stop in front of me. 'The sacrificial lamb.'

I kept quiet, holding his gaze as he run his tongue over his lips.

Hyperion stepped backwards, away from me, his eyes still fixed on mine. 'Who are you, what's your name?'

I didn't answer.

Hyperion smirked. 'Oh, ok, don't tell me,' he said, his golden eyebrows knitting together as he looked deep into my eyes. I felt myself falling into those raging pools of fire, felt the fingers of his mind probing mine.

'Hello Josh,' he said, as I felt his mind push me away and return me to the room. 'So, how did She get you to come and find me? I don't know you from Adam, although, to be honest, I don't really know Adam all that well, despite what the gossips say, but I digress.' He shrugged, then looked away as if he were in deep thought. 'I know...I know this,' he said, waggling his forefinger in the air. He stopped still, his head cocked to the side, a wide grin spreading across his face. 'Evie...that's why you're here! You're in love!' He clasped his hands to his chest. 'You're in love, although that should not be possible! All *very* intriguing, I must say.'

My heart leapt into my mouth at the mention of her name. How did he know?

'What's a matter, Josh? Don't you want to talk about it?' Hyperion stepped forward, placing his hand on my shoulder. I trembled under his touch. 'Is being apart from her breaking your heart that much?'

'Leave Evie out of this!' I spat, unable to ignore the heat building in the chamber any longer.

Hyperion stepped back, removing his hand quickly as if I had burnt him. 'But how can I?' he asked, 'Evie is now a part of this, whether you like it or not.'

'I broke the rules, not her. I saved her life. I have to pay, so leave her alone.'

Hyperion tapped his lips with his finger. 'I see where you're coming from, really I do, but,' he said, his head rocking from side to side, as though he was deliberating with himself, 'you see, you brought her into all of this when you saved her-'

'But, I saved her, she didn't ask-'

'I'm afraid it isn't that simple, Josh; Evie should've died but she didn't, because of you. And now she's sitting at home, doing whatever it is depressed teenagers usually do, when she should be fluttering around,' he said, flapping his hands in the air like wings, 'pretty as you like, collecting dead souls.'

'But-'

'No buts Josh,' he said, raising his hand to stop me, 'You know I speak the truth. Evie should be dead, serving her punishment for taking her own life, for committing that sin. You changed all that Josh. You pissed Death off.'

I stared into Hyperion's raging eyes, letting his words sink in, feeling the ball of dread in my gut twist. Had I become a part of something bigger, something happening between Death and Hyperion?

'Oh, Joshy, Sweetheart,' said Hyperion, stepping forward to pat me on my cheek, 'when are you going to wake up! You Angels of Death, so much sin and atonement, so much innocence, I do feel so sorry for you -'

'Don't be sorry for me!' I spat.

'But I do,' he replied calmly, his hand still resting on my cheek. 'Think about it. You're stripped of all emotions, of all memories, leaving you in a state of ignorance. Your Soul, left in a shell of your former self, rumbles on, atoning for a crime you don't even remember committing.' He threw his hands in the air. 'And they believe that this will bring you back to the fold and back to innocence?' He took a step back, and crossed his arms over his chest. 'But I ask you, Josh, what is the point of returning to innocence if we live in ignorance?'

'What has this got to do with Evie?'

'Don't you see?'

I shook my head.

'No, of course you don't.'

I tried to remain still as he leant forward. I could feel his breath on the side of my neck, could smell the metallic aroma of his skin. 'Death,' he whispered into my ear, 'has lied to you.'

I took a step backwards from him. 'How? How has She lied to me?'

'Consider this; where would you be now, if it wasn't for Her?'

'What?'

'Where would you be now? If She hadn't made you come here.'

'I'd be dead! That's where I would be. I broke the rules, I should be dead!'

I felt like a dog being prodded by a little boy with a big stick, and I didn't know how long I could keep a lid on my anger which was slowly uncoiling within me like a cobra. 'I should be dead,' I repeated, trying hard to keep the frustration from my voice.

'You are wrong. Even after your little misdemeanour, you didn't have to die.

'What?'

'Now bear in mind I'm only telling you this because I like you, because I consider anyone who pisses Death off to be a friend.' He put his burning arm around me but it felt cold to the touch, 'You didn't have to die, there was another option; She could've punished you by making you one of the Fallen.'

I shook him off and took a step backwards, my heart on fire with hope. 'You're lying-'

'No,' said Hyperion, his golden eyes pleading with me, 'I am the only one who is telling you the truth. You know that I am the Archangel of Wisdom?'

'That doesn't mean you-'

Hyperion shook his head, his hair of fire rippled around him. 'No Josh,' he said, moving forward, placing his hand on my arm, 'She has lied, manipulated you, and your love for Evie.' I felt his hand tighten on my arm. 'Do you not see? She's using you like a pawn in some twisted game of chess.'

'No!' I said, pulling my arm from Hyperion's hand. I stepped away, my knuckles turning white as I gripped the book he'd given me. I needed time to think, to work out what to believe. Who to believe.

'Within these walls lies the secret to you being with Evie, the key to unlocking that which has been purposely hidden from you; the Fallen, your means to being with Evie. I have told you that, I tell you the truth. Not Her!'

'You're trying to confuse me, to make me doubt-'

'Believe that if it makes it easier,' said Hyperion shrugging, 'But don't tell me I didn't warn you, or give you a way out. You can be with Evie, the information is out there if you are willing to take it. But I can see you are too much of a coward and would rather stay in the dark!'

'I don't believe you!' How could it be true?

'Believe me or don't. I couldn't give a damn either way. Your little love affair is of no importance to me!' he said. 'Now, I must be off, enjoy your reading.' His face lit up with a wide smile as he released his wings, ecstasy running down his spine.

I couldn't move, my eyes were transfixed by the beauty of his wings as they opened, a thousand shimmering feathers of fire. I imagined that this is how Hell felt. He formed a fist with his right hand, and before I had chance to react, he threw himself forward and punched the marble floor. The ground began to shake as fire bubbled, like molten lava, up through the hole.

'Don't do this,' I warned, struggling to keep the chaos raging inside me under control.

'What? This?' Hyperion boomed, as he pounded the floor again and again with his hand of gold.

Cracks of fire appeared in the floor and it was as if he were knocking through to Hell. There was a resounding crack as the ceiling fractured above us, sending large chunks of jagged marble raining down, distracting me just for the smallest of moments, and when I looked up again, Hyperion had gone, with only the smell of burnt flesh and destruction left behind in his wake.

But I could feel his imprint left on my flesh like a stain; it had penetrated through my skin.

What if Hyperion was right? Had Death lied to me? Could I really be with Evie as one of The Fallen?

The whole place was crumbling around me; I had to get out. And yet...

I frantically looked around. I looked at the leather book in my hands. Where would I find a book on The Fallen? I spun around on my heels, consumed by the need to find out. I ran down the corridor I had come from and back to the circular atrium, the ground splitting and hissing as I ran, the heat burning into the soles of my feet, and yet

I felt no pain. I was driven by something that knew no pain.

I rounded the corner, and found that the floor above me was now starting to slide through the hole I had made earlier. The whole building was unstable. I had to act fast before the whole of the Castel collapsed on top of me. I climbed over the piles of rubble trying to work out where I would find a book on the Fallen, but I didn't know where to start looking.

I turned around just as a huge rumble brought a large section of masonry down, setting off a chain reaction around the atrium as other large blocks crashed to the floor. It was no use, I had to get out of there.

I clutched the book against my chest. How could I have been so close and yet leave empty handed? But I had no choice, I had to run before the building claimed me. I took the only exit I could see and ran. And now that I was running I could not look back, even when I could feel the corridor collapsing behind me.

The dust was clawing at my lungs, drying my mouth out and making it difficult to breathe. How I hated being a freak. Half angel, half human; weak and feeble!

I fled down the corridor, my wings burning on my back, desperate to burst out and take me away from there. But I couldn't let them emerge; they would only hinder me in such a constricted space.

And then I saw light at the end of the tunnel. I ran straight for it, the air in my lungs burning in my chest. I flung myself through the opening and into the dawn, taking a good gulp of fresh air, and finally letting my wings explode from my back.

The pain ripped through my body as they burst violently through my skin. My mind went black and my body went limp. I fell forwards onto the cold damp floor. I scraped at the ground trying to regain control over my body, to fight the pain.

I took to the sky, not looking back until I reached the relative safety of the dome of Saint Peter's. I landed on the ornate dome for a brief respite from the pain. I folded my wings back, and turned to sit down on the apex, just below the spire. The view over Rome was now distorted, corrupted like the angel I had been sent to find. The Ponte Sant' Angelo, the bridge that used to run over the Tiber had fallen into the river, its Bernini angels lost to the churning waters. As the Castel continued to collapse, great chunks of masonry fell into the raging river with a boom, sending waves of discontent rolling down the Tiber, washing away anything in its path. Boats, trees, walls, all fell to the raging torrent.

Sirens blared from every direction as the chaos took hold, blue and white lights flashed as ambulances and the police rushed to the scene of the devastation. But I couldn't think about that now, my head was like the confusion unfolding before me on the streets of Rome; torn between guilt (for what I'd done in bringing this anarchy to pass) and my anger at myself, at Hyperion, at Death. I'd saved Evie, believed Death, and listened to Hyperion. But now what? Who was I to believe? Was Death really lying to me? Was I only some tiny pawn in a sick game between Her and Hyperion?

I sat, cross-legged, on the dome of Saint Peter's, the Castel Sant' Angelo destroyed. How many people had died today? I should've been used to death, to destruction, but my heart felt like lead inside me.

I couldn't look anymore. I didn't want to see my fellow Angels of Death arriving to take away the dead.

Instead I looked at the cover of the book still clasped in my hands. "The Apocalyptic Relics" read the golden

Angelic Script on the leather cover. I opened it and roared as fury ripped through me. The pages had been torn out, replaced instead by sheets of blank paper. One by one I grabbed the imposters from the cover and scrunched them up, throwing them away so that they cascaded down the dome like snow. Only one page from the original text remained, and over it, someone had scribbled the words "The Fallen", in thick red letters.

I ripped the page from the book, letting the cover clatter down the dome, and with a roar of defiance, I took off into the sky.

Josh

I wanted to see Death. I wanted Her to tell me Hyperion was wrong. I wanted to know the truth.

But no matter how much I raged at her, or how high I flew, She wouldn't see me. She wouldn't allow me to return to the Other Side.

I was left with nothing but the stormy sea of thoughts churning in my head.

What if Hyperion was right? Was Death lying to me? Could She have made me a Fallen? Could I really be with Evie?

What if...

What if the only way to find out was now lost to me, hidden under tons of rubble in Rome?

I stared at my reflection in the gilt mirror hanging on the wall of the apartment I'd managed to charm my way into. I hated what I'd had to resort to, what I'd become; a trickster, a shadow. My eyes were dull and lifeless, ringed by black, my face pale and gaunt.

I turned away, disgusted, and punched the wall, my anger wrapping me up in its violent arms.

But, in the depths of my madness, one thing still held true; my love for Evie.

I had tried so hard not think about her, to save myself the pain after saying goodbye, but now...now she seemed to be the only light in the dark. Although my wings had gone, the mark left on my back, as black as a tattoo, burned and throbbed with the thought of her. It was a pain that I now welcomed because it brought memories of Evie with it.

I imagined her reading on her window seat, her legs tucked under her, her fingers delicately playing with the silver key on the chain around her neck, her ebony hair pulled up into a ponytail. I tried to conjure in my mind the strawberry scent of her hair, the soapy aroma of her skin and dreamed of what it would be like to kiss those dusky pink lips.

But Hyperion's word intruded on my thoughts, like the ghosts of those left unburied; 'the Fallen, your key to being with Evie.'

I should've stayed away.

But that would've been like trying to catch snow when it already had fallen into the ocean.

I had to see her.

I ran into the night with only that thought in my mind.

I reached the dis-robed oak tree at the edge of the park, opposite her house. I would've stayed there as long as it took just to see her again, maybe then I would know what to do, who to trust?

I looked up at the waning moon, barely visible beneath the thick veil of cloud. If only I was still an Angel of Death, then I'd have been able to drift in the window and see her.

The screech of a fox pierced the silence as it scampered across the road, oblivious to my suffering.

And yet, the whole world suffered but I couldn't see it.

I was losing my mind.

Evie

The Sandman's magic wasn't working very well; I woke up early (again), before the birds had even started their winter chorus. I pulled my duvet over my head trying to block out the the sounds of morning, but it was no good, my mind was too alert, so I gave up and got out of bed. I looked out the window hoping that the snow had turned to ice and another day off school, but it was now nothing more than slush, clinging onto life in small pockets where it hadn't melted.

My stomach turned over, my heart thumped against my chest. I didn't want to go to school, I didn't want to face the day, and yet, when I looked around my room and felt the empty space pushing down on me, the absence of company and of sound, I didn't want to stay at home either. I didn't know where I belonged anymore, I was stuck in some sort of No Man's land.

In the end, I left the house early, defeated by the noisy silence.

Before long I found myself at the Old Bridge that straddled the river Tame, the scene of the "accident". It was the first time I'd been back since, and I didn't really know why I had returned; it wasn't as if I'd made a conscious decision to go there, but my feet, by some compulsion of their own, had brought me back. I walked to the centre of the bridge, the scene of the crime, driven by something deep inside, an aching for something I'd lost, or maybe it was something I'd never had. I don't know, but the ache was there, right at the bottom of my ribcage.

I stopped at the point where I'd jumped and looked out over the river. The willow tree still sighed at its bank, its long drooping branches still skimming the glass-like surface of the water, the spire of St John's silhouetted against the sky as the morning's sun began to bloom.

Life was still happening, right there in front of me.

And whatever it was that I'd lost, wasn't to be found here.

I watched the world go by, me stuck in the centre, on some kind of eternal pause, as everyone around me whizzed by like they were on fast forward. Everything was out of my control and their wasn't a thing I could do about it.

At school, Sam watched me like all day, scrutinising my every move, waiting for me to do what exactly? He was putting me on edge.

I sat in the middle of the art room, a large blank canvas in front of me, planning my piece on Sabre, my kick-ass warrior girl, the final piece on this theme before we started a new topic. I could feel Sam's eyes burning on the back of my neck so I turned around and caught him looking at me, a strange expression on his face. I pulled a face back at him, and mouthed the word "what?" but he just shook his head and turned away.

The art room was set on the upper floor of the main school building, a converted Victorian Workhouse, which was totally unsuitable light for painting but I loved it anyway. It was dark but full of charm with its exposed beams and heavy wooden work benches, dented and plastered with paint. The white washed walls were covered with giant canvases smeared in every colour, every texture and every theme you could think of. I loved it here, in my world of colour and dreams; it was the one place where I didn't feel a freak, the only place that I felt like I belonged. And on the wall, looking down at me, like a Guardian Angel, was a portrait I'd done of my father in pencil.

Miss Powell, the art teacher, glided over to me, a small pile of sketches in her paint splattered hands, her blonde hair long and wild. She always reminded me of The Lady of Shalott in the John William Waterhouse painting we'd studied in year nine.

'Ah, Evelyn, got anything for me?'

'Er, yes,' I said, moving the canvas in front of me to reach my sketches, 'there you go.'

'Thank you,' she said, looking through them, 'these are really good, you should be proud of them.'

She took a sharp intake of breath, and my stomach tensed.

'Evelyn, you could be an A-star student, but you need to make sure you attend classes and get your work in on time.'

I nodded my head but didn't say a word.

'Are you feeling better now?' she asked, clutching the sketches to her chest.

'Yes, thanks,' I said, but my words were fake and hollow.

'Okay, keep your attendance up because you don't want to make it any harder on yourself, okay? Lower sixth form is really important to build up your portfolio.' She turned to walk away and then stopped, turning back to face me. 'Oh, I forgot, this was left on my desk for you,' she said, giving me a small white envelope with my name scribbled on it.

'Thanks,' I said, taking it from her.

I waited for her to go before I slid my thumb under the corner of the envelope. It came away easily, as the glue was still slightly damp. The crisp white paper smelt of perfume or after shave, it was a floral scent which seemed really familiar, although I couldn't place from where. I unfolded the paper and read the short printed note.

Evelyn,

Sorry about the other day, I just didn't know what to do or what to say. The truth is, I've been thinking about you a lot since I found you at Christmas. If you feel the same way, meet me after school at the back of the basketball court,

Dex.

My heart seemed to jump into my throat as I read the words, then read them again. I folded the note up and dropped it in my bag.

The art lesson dragged. I tried not to think about meeting Dexter after school but my heart was racing, my mind imagining what could be.

What if, what if...

I couldn't quite get the composition right on my board and now it was just a mish-mash of pencil lines and rubbed out smudges. I'd have to white it over with paint and start again. My heart just wasn't in it. My heart nor my head. The lines just seemed to move on their own, to almost get up and move themselves across the canvas.

Waiting for home-time was like crawling down a very long, painfully rough road on my hands and knees. The bell went for lunch and I ran from the art room as fast as I could, deliberately avoiding Sam. I felt awful, he was my best friend but I couldn't talk. So many things were rolling around in my mind that I might just let it all spew out if I started speaking. But some things were only for me, and I didn't know if I could hold everything in my head.

I sat in the corner of the cafeteria picking at my egg mayo sandwich when Sam slipped into the red plastic chair in front of me.

'You okay?' he said, his eyebrow raised so far that I thought it might take off at any moment.

'Yeah,' I replied, not taking my eyes off the drying crust of the sandwich.

'Are you sure?' he said, putting his cold hand over mine to stop me picking.

'I said so, didn't I?' I didn't want to do this. Not now. Not today.

'You would tell me if there was anything wrong-'

'You know I would,' I said, looking into his eyes really hard without blinking. I tried sending him telepathic messages that I was telling the truth.

'We've been friends for so long Ev, I thought you could trust me-'

'What are you on about?' I said, trying to sound as nonchalant as possible, acting like I hadn't got the foggiest idea what he was talking about, whilst trying to contain the tide of my thoughts, like King Canute.

He sighed, looking at me like I was a naughty two year-old. 'The photo?'

'Oh,' I said, trying to sound as casual as possible, 'that.'

'Yeah, that. Care to explain?'

'Why?' Suddenly my hackles raised and my defences went up.

'Why? What do you mean, why? You try and kill yourself and you just sit there and say why?'

'What are you talking about, I have not tried to kill myself! If I had I would've made sure I'd finished the job properly,' I said, hating myself as the lies fell easily from my mouth. How had this chasm opened up in our friendship? 'That photo you're talking about is part of an art project thing I'm doing-'

'An art project? What art project? You really expect me to believe that?'

'Believe what you want,' I said, rising from my chair, 'people usually do anyway.' I dropped the sandwich on the plate, grabbed my bag and bounded to the toilets, trying to look as hurt as possible.

I stayed, locked in that toilet through all of lunchtime, listening to the traffic of girls coming and going, laughing, crying, vomiting. I suppose we all had our own issues to deal with. I used to be friends with a lot of those girls - Danni, Max and Sara - before all this happened, before I lost myself.

The bell went for Registration. I picked myself off the toilet lid, took a deep breath and strode out into the crowds with their painted faces and fake smiles.

'Hey,' said Sam as I emerged. 'I'm sorry,' he said, standing up from where he'd been leaning against the wall which was covered in careers posters. One was for the army. That sounded like a great idea, running away to join the army, to leave all this crap behind. Even better, I could've run away to the Foreign Legion.

God, he hadn't been waiting there all that time had he? 'It's okay,' I replied, the hate I felt for myself deepening with every word that came out of my mouth. 'There's no need to worry,' I said, looking intently into his eyes, 'I'm fine. Promise.' And when I said it like that, I almost believed it myself.

'Come on,' he said smiling, although the smile didn't quite reach his eyes as it usually did, 'We better get to Registration.'

After the register and class notices, Sam escorted me to history and I thought he might just haunt me until I told him the truth.

But that could never happen.

Like I said, that stuff was mine, and mine to keep.

The history room was bigger than the art room but just as dark, being on the floor below, and lit only by a few lights hanging from the ceiling and a large arched window cut in half by the floor, the point of which belonged to art. Replica suits of armour, a wooden guillotine, several polystyrene angels and stage props were scattered around the room, donated to the school by an old pupil, some famous actor or something. Today the screens that usually divided the room into three, had been pulled back so that a lecture could be given to us all. On the white board at the back of the class the words "Spain in the Reigns of Ferdinand and Isabella, 1474 -1516".

Amber was huddled next to Dexter, stroking his hair like he was a pet dog. I couldn't help thinking how tragic she looked, like she was trying to keep him on a leash; if he were mine, I wouldn't be doing that.

I pulled out my pad and biro, and began doodling whilst I waited for the lecture to begin.

Soon the page was covered in lots and lots of eyes; some big, some tiny, ones with huge eyelashes, other with none, some were just the irises, and they were all staring back at me.

'Evelyn,' someone said, a cold sneering voice trying to break into my consciousness. 'Evelyn? Earth to Evelyn!'

I suddenly realised I was still in class and the voice was talking to me. I looked up to see the whole of the class staring back at me. Mr Partridge was standing right in front of my desk and he looked like he'd just swallowed a wasp. 'Sorry Sir, I-'

'Back with us now?' he said, his big black eyes scrutinising the paper in front of me. 'So what is more important than your A-levels? Let's share it with the class, shall we?' Mr Partridge picked up the paper and began to flap it in the air like he was having a fit. 'Whilst Evelyn Anderson is, as we all can see, accomplished at drawing eyes on scrap pieces of paper, I don't think that skill is going to get her very far in life is it?

'It is interesting, is it not, Ms Anderson, that the symbol that you have chosen to draw represents a person's inner vision, their spiritual sight and higher knowledge. Sadly, I think this is lacking in you, is it not? That's why there's a "der" in Anderson, after all.' The class erupted with laughter.

Although my head was telling me not to, my eyes instinctively sought out those of Dexter and Amber. Dexter was staring straight ahead, Amber draped over him like some grotesque fur collar, her eyes alight with laughter, her brown hair swaying as she shook her head.

But Dexter wants to see me after school. I concentrated on that thought and stuck two fingers up at her in my head.

There was a loud slap of paper as Mr Partridge threw my pad back at me.

'I suggest, Ms Anderson, that if you want to pass your A-levels you at least have the common decency to listen in class. Now, where was I? Yes,' he said, putting his fat yellow finger to his lips, 'that's right, the Spanish Inquisition. A very useful tool as many Moors and Jews….'

How I hated Mr Partridge at that moment.

I ripped the front page off my pad, screwed it up, then dropped it on the table in front of me. I sat upright, my eyes staring straight ahead. Anyone looking at me would have thought that I was paying attention to Mr Partridge's wonderful lesson. Now and again I scribbled a few words down, those that had entered my brain quite by accident, although nothing was really soaking in at all.

It felt like dying, from the inside out.

Finally the bell rang for end of school. I grabbed my pad, pen and book and stuffed them into my bag and darted for the door. I couldn't talk to Sam and I certainly wasn't going to look at Amber. I couldn't, I may as well have written "I'm meeting Dexter after school" on the white board.

I bounded into the nearest toilet, giving Amber time to leave, shutting myself in the farthest cubicle. I sat on the toilet lid, my stomach churning, my hands sweaty. I rubbed the palms of my hands up and down my jeans to dry the sweat off, my legs bouncing up and down as I counted the minutes.

How was I going to hold it together and have a conversation with him?

Once the chaos had died down outside, I left the cubicle and made my way over to the basketball pitch at the back of the school. My stomach was rolling and I felt sick with anticipation.

The sky was darkening quickly, the sinking sun hidden by a curtain of dark cloud. The bitter wind howled and raged as it tore across the pavement, cutting through me to the bone. I slipped away from the crowds and headed towards the out buildings containing the basketball court.

I was alone.

My body had been dull to anything that was going on outside of my own self for such a long time and yet now I shuddered as I felt something dark and dangerous lurking in the air. I wrapped my arms around my chest and concentrated on getting to Dexter.

I turned the corner. Amber and Sara were leaning up the wall, sheltering themselves from the biting wind.

My heart seemed to stop beating. My panic rose into my throat where it wriggled and squirmed as it tried to scratch its way out. It was telling me to run. Run. Do something!

And then it fell back into my stomach, landing heavily, taking my breath away as the truth became clear. How stupid had I been to believe Dexter had wanted to see me?

I'd been set up.

I was burning up, despite the cold, and little pearls of sweat were beading on my palms. My heart rolled in my chest and I couldn't breathe. I thought I was going to pass out.

Keep walking, I told myself, keep those legs moving one on front of the other. Focus on that, nothing else, just make sure those legs keep moving.

I kept my head down, my eyes glued to the floor.

I started to pass them, the panic thumping my chest and tears building up at the back of my throat and behind my eyes. Don't cry. DO NOT CRY! No one was ever going to see me cry. I wasn't going to give them that, they taken too much of me already.

'What's a matter Evelyn?' asked Amber. Her manicured nails dug into my shoulder and she spun me around to face her. I couldn't help it, I hadn't any energy left to fight.

'Ah, look Sara, she's going to cry!'

'She is as well....Oh bless her!' said Sara, her baby-blue eyes full of pity and amusement.

My chest felt like it was being squeezed by two giant hands. The panic was becoming too strong, rising within me like a tidal wave and any minute it would come crashing down and would knock me off my feet.

'As if,' said Amber, 'Dexter would be interested in a skank like you.'

She shoved me backwards and I hit the wall.

The world was crashing down around me.

'Is there a problem ladies?' The voice was electric, shocking me back to life. I looked up to see a guy stood in front of us dressed only in a black tee-shirt and jeans, his hair scruffy and as black as the night.

'No problem,' giggled Sara, twirling her blond curls in her fingers, 'no problem at all!'

The stranger stepped forward and placed his hand on my shoulder. His touch sent a tremor through my body. My heart jolted. I took a gasp of air.

'Are you alright?'

I nodded weakly. 'I'm fine.' I said, only just managing to form words. 'Just not feeling...too well.' And I didn't. I thought I was going to be sick.

'No, you don't look so good,' he said, taking my face in his cold hand and tilting it towards him. His touch made my body tingle.

I looked up. His eyes were the strangest but most beautiful things I'd ever seen; a rainbow of light trapped in a diamond. Warmth flooded through me, and I lost what little train of thought I had. Those eyes. I was sure I'd seen them before. They were pulling me in. Holding me.

'Hey, come on, I'll take you home,' he said, wrapping his arm firmly around my back. He leant into me, his warm breath kissing the side of my face. 'Don't worry,' he whispered, 'I'm not going to hurt you. I just want to get you out of here, ok?'

I nodded. I couldn't think straight at all. I was being moved forward, but it felt like I wasn't moving at all.

'I'm warning you,' screeched Amber, to my back, 'you come anywhere near me, or Dexter again, I swear I will fucking kill you!'

'At least you'd do it properly,' shouted Sara, before they both squealed with laughter.

My mind was swimming away from me, my insides were jelly.

'Maybe we should get you warmed up first, you're shaking. Do you fancy a coffee or something?'

I didn't respond, lost in the fog of my own thoughts.

'Okay, don't worry,' I heard him say, 'we'll find somewhere to warm you up.'

The next thing I knew I was sitting in a booth at a fast food restaurant with a steaming cup of coffee in front of me. I was vaguely aware that my arms were clamped around my body, my legs bouncing up and down under the table.

I fixed my gaze on the broken edge of the coffee lid, desperately trying not to look at the stranger opposite me.

There was something about him, something that I couldn't quite put my finger on, that made me feel like I'd known him forever. A faint recollection of something, a sense of deja vu maybe? It was freaking me out. How could I have known him? Surely I'd be able to place those eyes if I'd seen them before, wouldn't I?

'Are you warming up now?' he asked.

I nodded, and grabbed my cup with both hands. I couldn't look at him; I was too scared. Not of him exactly, but the feelings that were surfacing inside me. They were becoming too loud, too scary to acknowledge, and I knew, that if I looked into those eyes, he'd pull me in again and those feelings would just become even louder.

'I'm sorry,' he said, reaching a hand out to touch me. He must've heard me sucking in my breath because he withdrew it quickly as he thought better of it, 'I never meant to freak you out...I just...I just couldn't leave you there.'

'It's okay,' I said. I took the lid off my coffee and swirled it around the cup. 'You're not freaking me out,' I lied.

'That's good to know,' he replied, laughing weakly, 'I don't make a habit of picking up.' his voice trailed off, lost to his own thoughts.

'What?' I said, 'Picking up what?' Anger rose in me. Where did that come from? I raised my head to challenge him, but all thought was lost as my eyes locked on to his. They pulled me in, stealing my words.

'Are you sure you're okay?' he asked, reaching out to touch me again.

I pulled my hands away quickly but his fingers brushed my skin. His touch was intense, too much for my awakening body to deal with.

I hadn't felt anything for so long and now...now his touch was making everything really loud and too real. What was I supposed to do with it? In one fluid motion I grabbed my bag from the floor and pushed my chair backwards.

'I'm sorry,' I said, standing up, making sure that I didn't look into his eyes again, 'I've got to go.' I spun on my heels, knocking the coffee over the table, but I couldn't look back, I had to get out.

'Thanks,' I mumbled, 'and sorry.'

I ran out of the restaurant.

'I can walk you home!' he called after me.

Outside rain was now pelting down. It quickly soaked through my jacket to my skin. The cold was biting and yet I didn't want to go home. I didn't know where I wanted to be, where I belonged.

I wandered the cold streets, my mind floating above me like it belonged to someone else, and all the time I kept replaying everything in my head, over and over again...I will fucking kill you...As if Dexter would be interested...I'll fucking kill you...And the stranger, the stranger with the rainbow eyes. It ran like a play in my head, like it had happened to someone else.

Somehow I found myself at home.

Home; that was such a strange word that should conjure up feelings of belonging, or warmth, of love, and yet, for me, it just made me feel even more lost.

With nowhere else to go, I let myself in.

I went into the kitchen and looked at the clock on the wall, its hands counting down the seconds and I could feel them slipping by with my life.

I dropped my bag on the floor and staggered up the stairs. I stripped and stepped into the shower, in the dark. The red hot water burnt my flesh, blasting me clean. I staggered out of the cubicle and crawled into bed, still wringing wet. Pulling the covers over my head, I prayed for a peaceful night, for the shadows to leave me alone and not taunt me.

And for once, the night was kind to me; it cradled me to sleep, letting me stay there, untroubled until my alarm bleeped at seven in the morning.

I felt different, like I, I mean what made me me ,my essence, was fluctuating in some sort of limbo. I didn't want to get up, but I didn't particularly want to stay in bed but it seemed as if my whole body had stopped working. I felt like stone, stuck in my bed, unable to move. But as I lay there, my hand lying on my chest, I felt my heart beating inside me.

And I knew something had to give.

The need for change pulled at my insides.

I'd had enough of being comfortably numb.

Josh

I leaned over the bridge and looked out at the river. I was stood at the spot where Evie had jumped, the place where everything had changed. I was feeling more miserable than ever as the rain tumbled down, washing everything but me clean.

I'd been watching Evie for days now, following her around like some love sick puppy, despising myself for how pathetic I was, and the longer Death kept me waiting, the more pitiful I was becoming. Why wouldn't Death just take me, deliver me from this madness?

My only redeeming quality had been my determination to stay away from Evie, my resolution to stay in the shadows. But now that resolve lay in tatters, trampled under my own big feet.

I couldn't help myself, seeing those girls taunting her, how was I supposed to walk away from that?

And yet, now I wasn't so sure.

What had I done?

The image of my dissolved wings, scorched into the flesh on my back like a brand, burned with the fire of my thoughts. The feel of her flesh lingered on my fingertips, the smell of her skin on mine.

I didn't know what I was supposed to do, what I should be doing with these feelings that were pulling me in different directions; wanting, no needing her, like the air we breathe, and yet not wanting to get close to her because I was under a death sentence.

And what was the point of it all anyway? Evie didn't know me, couldn't bear to look at me. Why couldn't I just stay away?

I deserved the pain as punishment.

The clock tower of St John's began to chime nine o'clock. I turned away and headed back over the bridge, trying to hammer my thoughts out with every heavy footstep.

This was Hyperion's fault, seducing me with those lies!

But, then, what if he was right? What if I could become a Fallen? Maybe, just maybe...

I needed to see Death. I was calm now, not full of anger after being taunted by Hyperion. She would have to see me. I'd done what She'd wanted; I'd reminded him of his obligations, now I'd go and see Her, talk to her, appeal to her better nature.

I headed back to my apartment, grabbed the lone sheet of paper I had kept from the book Hyperion had given me, the words "The Fallen" scrawled over it in red. I'd show Her that and then, perhaps, She'd tell me what it all meant.

I climbed up to the roof of the apartment block. I looked up at the sky and released my wings, let the pain rip through me as they erupted from my back. The bitter sweetness of it engulfed me, almost bringing me to my knees as pain transformed into beauty.

I stretched my wings out, testing them; they felt light and ripe for flight, so I launched myself into the sky.

She would see me.

She would have to listen to me.

The earth rapidly disappeared as I ascended, the clouds, the sky, all blending into one as I climbed higher. Water droplets clung to my skin as I burst through the atmosphere and into the blanket of stars behind it. The darkness surged forward, snuffing out the stars one by one, caressing me with what felt like a thousand hands stroking my flesh, massaging my aching bones.

'Josh,' She called to me through the dark. 'Welcome home,' She said, as Her cold lips found mine.

I turned my face away. 'I have done as you asked. I have found Hyperion and reminded him of his obligations.'

'Oh, why so angry, Josh? What have I done to deserve this?' She asked me, through the darkness, her fingers tracing the arch of my back.

'He gave me this,' I said, holding up the single page.

Death dropped her cloak of invisibility and stepped out of the darkness, her naked flesh covered only by the faintest wisps of the universe. Her beauty was breath taking. I took a sharp intake of breath, but I hated myself for letting Her see, for letting Her think there could be anyone but Evie.

She smiled at me, pleased at my mistake. She bit her bottom lip, as she moved in closer, the thinnest tendril of universe between our bodies. 'And what is that?'

'A page from a book he gave me,' I said, pulling away from her.

Death pouted. 'Does this feel like cheating?'

'I would never-'

She smiled, a look of amusement playing across her face as She ran her hand down my chest, making me shiver. She leaned forward and whispered into my ear, 'We'll see.'

Suddenly the air turned to ice, the cold instantaneously penetrating through my skin to my bones.

'So,' said Death, 'what have we here?' She took the page from me, letting her fingers brush against mine for a moment longer than they should have.

She looked at the paper. I watched as anger flashed in her eyes. Her face snapped up, her eyes narrowing into slits as She studied me. 'Where did you get this? Are you playing some sort of game?'

'No. I told you, Hyperion gave it to me. I followed him to the Forbidden Library at the Vatican. I reminded him of his obligations and then he gave me a book-'

'What book?'

'I don't know, he'd ripped it apart, replaced the pages with blank sheets, except for that one,' I said, pointing at the paper.

'Did you happen to see what this book was called?'

'No, I-'

'Where's the rest of it?'

'In Rome, I dropped it-'

'And yet you have this page? Why?'

I shrugged. 'I told you, that was the only page with anything on.'

Death stared at me in silence, gathering more of the universe around her, obscuring her naked body. 'What did he want with Obadiah?'

'He wanted to know how he could cleave his Arkhe-'

'Cleave his Arkhe, his celestial music?'

I nodded. 'Yes, that's why Obadiah told you about him.'

'He didn't tell me about Hyperion's desire to cleave his music.' Death rubbed her chin with her hand. 'I suppose that's why you found him at the Forbidden Library,' she said to herself, 'He was after the Necrodemonicon?'

'Obadiah sent him there, then contacted you-'

'Did he find it?'

'What?'

'The Necrodemonicon?'

I shrugged. 'I don't know. If he did, I didn't see him with it-'

'But he still had his music?'

'Yes, but it sounded strange, like nothing I've ever heard before.'

'And how did he look?'

'His aura was black around the edges, like it had been in a fire-'

'Yes, yes. But how did he *look*?'

'His eyes were raging with madness and I noticed he had jagged cuts running across his stomach, other than that, I don't know.' I watched as Death's face contorted with frustration. 'What do you want me to say?' I said, holding my hands up, 'You told me to remind him of his obligations and I've done that.'

'Indeed,' She said. There was a subtle change of atmosphere and I noticed her face soften a little. 'It seems that Hyperion's tiresome God-like tendencies are becoming a bit of a problem,' She said, 'You've done well, Josh.' She stepped forward and put her hand on my shoulder, 'Go and visit Evie, put a smile back on your face, you'll need it.'

'What do you mean?' I asked, shaking her hand from my shoulder. There was something about her voice, her choice of words.

'I'm afraid the game's changed, Josh, and I'm going to need you fully refreshed if we have any chance of stopping him.'

'But you said, if I reminded him of his obligations-'

'I have said a lot of things, but things change. Now go back to Evie, spend some time with her, put a smile on that miserable face of yours,' She said, flicking me away like a fly. 'I need to work out my next move.'

'What are The Fallen?' I asked. 'Hyperion told me-'

'Nothing that you need to worry your pretty little head about,' She said, dismissing me with a patronising pat on my head.

'What are they? Can I become one? If I do this for you?'

Death smiled at me, a patronising look of disbelief. 'There is only so much of your insolence I will put up with,' She said. 'Do not think for one minute you're not expendable, and what will happen to poor Evie then?'

'So?'

'So?' asked Death, her eyes narrowing into slits, reminding me of a serpent.

'So, if I do this for you, will you consider making me a Fallen?'

Death threw her head back and cackled. 'Oh Josh, you are so naive. Of course you can't become one of The Fallen-'

'Why? Why can't I, if I do whatever you ask, it's the least-'

She raised her hand, 'Stop!'

'But the page, Hyperion has written it on the page, it has to mean something.'

Her eyes now blazed with a new fire, the destructive crone clearly visible underneath her pale white skin. 'It means nothing! Hyperion is playing with you.' She paused, composing Herself before continuing. 'You were never a pure angel. An Angel of Death is a made entity, made because you sinned in your human life. It is this sin which prevents you from becoming a Fallen. Only a true, pure angel has a place to fall from.'

At Her words, hope left my body with the air from my lungs.

Death put her arms around me, pulling me in close to her. I could smell her sickly sweetness and I wanted to vomit.

'Josh, you took your own human life,' She cooed into my ear, 'Not only that, you deprived me of Evie, of a new angel to serve me. Do you really think I could ever forgive your disregard, your complete lack of respect for me?' She pulled away. 'You will do as I ask,' She said, 'Or you will pay the price. Then again, you're going to pay the price

anyway.'

Josh

Madness had possessed me, invading my body like a poison, preventing me from thinking clearly. Death was lying to me, She had to be. Did She really think that telling me I couldn't be a Fallen would make me do Her bidding? Did She think leaving a death sentence hanging over my head would be enough?

I wasn't going to be Her puppet anymore and I certainly wasn't going to help Her stop Hyperion. What was the point? There was nothing in it for me, nothing to make me do it.

She could destroy me, it didn't matter, I'd got nothing left to live for anyway.

The number three bus pulled into its stop and Evie climbed aboard. I followed after her, intoxicated by the sweet smell of her perfumed skin. I flashed a smile at the driver and walked straight past - without even a murmur of protest from him - and took up a seat at the back of the bus.

Evie was near the front, nursing her grey messenger bag on her lap, her face turned towards the window, looking out onto the grey morning. My wings raged under my skin, desiring release, agitated by the electrical pulses racing through my body, knowing that I was so close to her, and yet, as the cliche goes, so far away. A war was erupting in my soul, a fight between my reason and my desire, and the physical pain I felt when I was near her. The physical pain that made me feel alive.

I would make her notice me, despite what I'd promised myself. She would have to see me!

Evie turned around, her ebony hair falling over her face like a veil. She brushed it back and looked up at me and I watched as her face changed from shock to confusion. She quickly turned back to face the front.

Why wouldn't she see me? I looked down at my lap, watching my knuckles turn white as I gripped my legs.

I looked up, catching her emerald eyes staring back at me, and the breath caught in my throat. Her features softened and I think she recognised me, but she looked away again. Sliding down into her seat, she pulled her hood over her head.

The bus pulled into a stop and Evie suddenly darted for the door, taking me off-guard. The bus started pulling away from the stop as I stood up. Evie was peering at me through the grimy window, a look of horror (or was it anger?) on her face.

I rushed to the front of the bus. 'Sorry, can you let me off?' I asked, flashing another charming smile at the driver. He rolled his eyes, but applied his brake anyway. The bus grinded to halt, the doors opened and I stepped off.

'What's your problem?' said Evie, coming to a halt in front of me, her eyes blazing with a fire that I hadn't seen in such a long time that it almost didn't seem to fit her anymore. But something, a long lost memory, was picking at my mind, trying to break through the wall of ice. But I couldn't quite grasp it, it was too far away.

'What was that about?'

'I-'

'Why did you keep calling me on the bus?'

'I-'

'How do you even know my name?' she said, throwing back her hood. I caught her delicious scent on the breeze.

'I-' What could I say, what could I tell her? That I knew her in ways that no one else could, or ever would? That I'd watched her as she'd cried herself to sleep, seen her in her most darkest of moments? If only I could tell her that I'd saved her all those long nights ago. Would she even have believed me?

'Thank you for helping me out last night, but now you are, 'but she stopped as her eyes locked onto mine.

'I'm sorry...' I felt my heart rip apart. I stuffed my hands into my jeans pockets. 'I wasn't calling you-'

'So you're not following me?' she said, defiantly, like she wanted a fight.

'No. I'm going into town and got on the bus and saw you. I did recognise you from last night, but I wasn't going to speak. That's it.' I shrugged, my hands still deep in my pockets.

Evie stood there silent for a moment, her eyes staring into mine and slowly I saw the fight in them disappearing.

'Honestly,' I said, dying inside as I lied to her. 'I'm sorry if I've upset you.' I never want to upset you.

She sighed, her shoulders slackened, but her eyes, her eyes never left mine. And I didn't want them to.

'No,' she said, 'it's me...I'm the one who should be sorry...I just don't know what's happening to me anymore.'

She looked at the floor, and shuffled her feet. 'I just don't know,' she said, looking up and off into the distance.

'It's ok,' I said, wanting to close the space between us, wanting to sweep her up in my arms.

'Look, I don't want to be rude but I've got to get to school.' She looked back up at me again, and I could see the pain etched in her eyes, dulling the green.

A storm ripped my soul apart.

'I'll walk with you,' I said, quickly adding, 'if you want?'

She smiled, but it didn't reach her eyes. 'It's okay.'

'Where do you go? Riverside?' I asked. When she nodded, I added, 'I'm going that way, anyway.' I shouldn't have lied, I should've been a better person. She made me want to be a better person.

'Okay.'

'So, I'm Josh,' I said, begging for her to take notice of me, 'And?'

'Oh, I'm Evelyn,' she said, looking up at me again, 'Evelyn Anderson.'

'Hi Evie,' I said, smiling weakly, feeling my heart beat quicken as her name slipped off my tongue. I was so close to her that I could hear her heart pumping the blood around her body, could feel the invisible line that anchored me to her. All around me was electric, and I could feel every nerve in my body tingling. I was on overload. It was taking me all my time to just breathe, to work through my pain and desire. My thoughts were tangling in my head, and I couldn't form them into words.

Was she feeling the same?

Finally I managed a weak, 'So what happened the other night?'

I felt her shoulders tense, her arms clamp down at her side. 'Nothing...really.'

'Who was that crazy brunette?'

'Amber. Amber Staunton,' she replied, shrugging, 'I suppose that explains why you're talking to me-'

'No,' I said, 'no, I'm not talking to you because...no.' I shook my head, horrified at the unspoken meaning behind her words.

We reached the school gate. 'So, this is me,' she said.

I put my hand on her shoulder, the touch sent a heady mix of electrical desire and the pain of a thousand knives through me. 'Are you going to be okay?'

She turned slightly. 'Yes, I'm going to be okay.'

She turned and walked into the school without looking back once.

My eyes did not leave her until she had disappeared through the glass doors of Riverside Academy. But I could feel her presence, her mark on my soul, like a fingerprint.

Was that it then?

I dragged myself away from the school gates and headed back to my apartment, my heart torn in two.

No, she didn't feel the same.

Evie

What was I doing? What was I thinking?

I let the stranger walk me to school, trying to avoid those beautiful eyes that sucked me in and made everything far too loud.

No one was nice to me, except for Sam, and look how I treated him. I didn't deserve it.

I left the stranger at the school gates and didn't look back. I just couldn't deal with all that, not now I'd decided what I was going to do.

I kept my eyes on the floor and slunk past the cafeteria, past the theatre and down the steps to the nurse's office in the bowels of the school.

I wanted to turn and run, to hide away somewhere, but I knew I had to keep going forward.

I couldn't go on like this.

It was a matter of life or death; if I couldn't slay the beast inside me then I would die. Simple as that.

I sat on the stained chair outside the nurse's office, just waiting, pulling at a frayed thread on the sleeve of my hoodie. I fidgeted in the chair, played with the clasp on my bag, bounced my legs up and down, wrapped my arms around my chest, unwrapped them, pulled at the thread on my hoodie again.

Time had stood still and I was finding it increasingly difficult to fight the urge to run.

I looked down the corridor, there was no one there, no one had seen me, and no one would see me leave. I grabbed my bag just as the nurse opened the office door. She shuffled out, drowning in a sea of black cardigan. She had a warm, kind look about her that worried me. Like I said, I wasn't good around nice.

'Ah, hello. Evelyn Anderson isn't it?'

I smiled and nodded.

'Come in, ' she said, holding the door open.

I stood up but my legs were trembling so much that I didn't think I would be able to get them to work. I took a deep breath and entered her office that smelled of bleach and polish.

'Take a seat,' she said.

I sat on the plastic seat, huddled next to her beech desk, and stared at the large couch in front of me, covered in what looked like oversized toilet tissue. The end of the blue roll was perched at the bottom of the bed.

'Okay,' she said, tapping away at her computer, 'Evelyn Anderson, what's your date of birth?'

'Seventh of November, nineteen-ninety-five.'

She looked over to me, her smiling eyes looking over the top of her glasses, 'So what can we do for you?'

My mouth was dry, I didn't know whether I'd be able to form the words. 'I need help. I can't seem to shake whatever it is.'

'So what's been the problem?'

'Er…' Where did I start? I see shadows laughing at me at night, I'm mad, I can't think straight. I tried to kill myself.

'I've been tired a lot lately, probably just all the study though, everyone gets like that. Don't they?'

'Okay,' she said, her fingers tapping on the keyboard, 'Anything else?'

'Er…' I think I'm going nuts? 'I passed out the other day-'

'Are you eating properly? You do know that a balanced diet is essential.'

I shrugged.

The nurse suddenly stopped tapping and looked back over to me. Her glasses had slipped to the bottom of her nose. 'You're not pregnant are you?'

My face went into spasm just at the thought of that. 'Oh, God no.'

'Are you sure? It's amazing what some girls believe.'

I shrunk back into my chair and flung my hand up to stop her. 'No. I can't be, not unless it was an immaculate conception.'

She studied me for a minute, trying to work out whether I was telling the truth or not. She turned back to her computer screen. 'Okay,' she said, 'let's do your blood pressure.'

She placed the pressure pad around my arm and started to pump it up. I hate that sensation where it cuts off the blood to your hand and your arm feels like it's going to explode.

'I feel like that,' I said. It sort of just tumbled out, like half of my internal conversation had suddenly sprouted legs and had walked out of my mouth all on its own.

'Excuse me?' said the nurse. She stopped pumping the machine and just looked at me.

'I feel like my hand now, when you've stopped the blood flow and it feels numb and tingly.' Yep, my words were fleeing from me.

'You feel numb? What do you mean?'

'Like someone has filled me up with anaesthetic, and now, now I don't know how I feel.' A big fat tear drop fell onto my arm lying across the desk. Why was I crying? No one was supposed to see me cry. I couldn't even get that right.

'How long have you felt like this?'

I shrugged.

'Have you ever…' the nurse looked troubled, maybe even embarrassed. 'Have you ever cut yourself?'

I shook my head.

'What about suicidal thoughts?' she asked, placing her hand on my arm. 'Have you had any of those?'

'No,' I lied. That was mine to keep.

'Okay,' said the nurse, relaxing in her chair a little. She reached up to grab a sheet of paper from the plastic file on her desk. 'Can you fill this in for me?' She handed me the sheet of paper with a list of statements on it. 'Don't take too long but read through them, tick the boxes that apply to you, but don't think too hard about it, okay?'

She gave me a pen, stood up and tapped me on the shoulder. 'I'll be back in a minute,' she said before she left the room.

I looked at the questions on the paper. Did I feel like impending doom was about to befall me every day? No. Did I feel like...

Was this what my life consisted of now? A series of boxes?

A bit fat blob of saltiness plopped in the middle of the paper. It splattered out like blood. I squirmed. I hated blood, just the thought of it. That's why I'd decided to jump off the bridge. I could do that.

Or maybe I couldn't.

Something in the long list of things I couldn't get right.

I put the pen down just as the nurse re-entered the room.

'Okay, let's have a look now, shall we?' she said placing a gentle hand on my shoulder. 'Don't look so worried.' Her tone had changed with me, like I was a delicate ornament that could be broken just by words.

She took the piece of paper. I could see her eyes tracing across the boxes, tracing across my life. She sighed and looked up at me. She took off her glasses, folded them up and placed them on the desk. 'There's nothing to worry about but I would like you to go and see your GP. Do you think you could do that as soon as possible for me?'

I nodded, confused. What had she seen in those little boxes of my life?

As if she heard what I was thinking she spoke gently, as if her words could soothe away my troubles. 'I think you may have depression and from what these tell me,' she said, pointing at the piece of paper, 'a touch of anxiety too. It's nothing to be ashamed of. A lot of people suffer.'

She smiled at me kindly and I thought I was going to explode.

'It might help if you had counselling, just talking about it can sometimes help. If you wanted you could do that here-'

'No,' I said, cutting her off. It would somehow get around school that I was seeing a counsellor. People thought I was a freak anyway, why would I want to go and advertise the fact that I'd now officially lost the plot? 'I'll see my GP,' I said in barely more than a whisper. I stood up, grabbed my coat and bag and shuffled towards the door.

'Go home, make the appointment, and we'll see you back here in a week's time.'

I nodded and quickly escaped. Escaped from the sterility, from the kindness, from her.

I don't remember much of the journey home; I spent most of it with my head down looking at the frayed thread of my hoodie, too ashamed to look up in case someone saw through me, saw what I'd become.

My head felt like it was going to implode as I thought about all these crazy scenarios. My mother? What would happen to me if she died? What would happen to me if she died whilst on holiday? What would happen if she got married to Dan then died? Crazy, stupid questions, but I couldn't help thinking about them, and the more I thought about them, the more confused I became, The more confused I became the more I felt crazy and out of control, like I was hurtling towards a wall, in a train travelling at one-hundred miles-per-hour.

I was out of control.

I stumbled through the front door and dropped my bag down on the floor and ran upstairs for a hot, hot shower. I cranked the shower up. Maybe, just maybe, I could purge myself of the madness.

I crawled out of the shower, my skin red-raw. Even that didn't make me feel any better now. Still wet, I crawled into bed and waited for the demons to come. And they came, laughing and pointing their fingers at me, old faces laughing with the new demons I seemed to be collecting.

Sleep took its time, but I still woke really early the next day, at six in the morning, alert and unable to sleep despite the fact my body was still stone-tired. But I didn't get out of bed. Instead, I just lay there, under the duvet, trying to pretend that life was not happening. I don't know how long I just lay there, thinking about the knives in the kitchen and how I might hurt myself with one without knowing. My body was broken, my mind shattered.

There was a banging of doors downstairs. My heart jumped in my chest, I stopped breathing, but I couldn't move.

And then Aunt Celia was at my bedroom door, her face like thunder. 'Come on get up!' she said, putting her hand across her face as if to protect herself from some kind of bad smell. 'Get up!' she screeched, 'I need you downstairs. NOW!' She turned around, sweeping from the room. I heard her footsteps pounding down the stairs.

Somehow, I really don't know how, I managed to get my legs to work and stumbled down the stairs after her.

I entered the living room just as she threw open the curtains, the light was blinding, stinging my eyes.

'You haven't been skulking around here all week long have you? Why aren't you at school? Your face is like a wet weekend,' she said, turning to face me, her mouth curled in a sneer of disgust. 'You need to pull yourself together!'

Reminds me of that crap joke: Doctor, Doctor, I feel like a pair of curtains and the doctor replies 'Come on man, pull yourself together. 'I mean, what does "pull yourself together" even mean?

Still, she continued to rant. 'Do you want your mom to get into trouble?'

'No.' I sounded sulky, like a petulant child.

'Good,' get this place tidied up, 'she's coming home tomorrow. It's been a tough few years for her Evelyn, she doesn't need you going off on one too.'

I looked at Celia's face, her red hair scraped back in a ponytail, her horsey mouth, her big white teeth dazzling against her orange fake tan and she made me want to puke.

'Okay?' I hear her finish. I nodded my head dutifully.

'What time does her plane land?' I ask, not because I care, but because I know this is what's expected of me.

Celia gave me a you should already know this type of look. 'Six. Make sure this place is tidied up and Evelyn -'

'Yeah?'

'It would be good if you could stop thinking of yourself for one moment and be pleased for her. Losing your dad like that, and then your Gran, you know.'

I nodded my head. Maybe it was my fault dad died. Everything was my fault.

'It might be good to get her an engagement card, that is, if you can manage to get yourself out of the house.'

'Okay.' So he had asked her to marry him then.

And as quick as she had arrived, she had left. Like a tornado. And I was stuck in the calm after the storm, the memory of it lingering in the air.

I dumped myself on the sofa. Everyone seemed to be happy apart from me. Why could I not be happy? What was wrong with me? Was I such a terrible daughter?

Pathetic, pathetic, pathetic! I hit the side of my head hard, trying to knock out the despair. But it didn't work.

I looked out of the window at the clouds floating by peacefully, untroubled by nothing but the wind. What it must be like to be free. Sometimes I wished I could be a cloud floating in the sky, not having to worry about being a freak, about not feeling anything. Or a bird. To be able to fly away, to fly high above the clouds.

I felt a wave of sadness wash over me, my heart was like lead in my chest. But I could sense a change in myself.

I was at a crossroads. But I didn't know which road to take.

Evie

I sat in the dark, the blackness punctuated now and again by the streak of headlights from passing cars. Cassie's voice cut through the silence as the answering machine clicked on.

'Hi Hun, just gone to Celia's to show her the ring. I'll tell you all about it tomorrow; I've got so many ideas that I don't know where to start. I won't be back until late, so don't wait up.'

I couldn't believe that she'd gone and done it again, and put me at the bottom of her list. But then, I was only her daughter.

If she'd abandoned me - left my life for good - it would be different, but instead she'd abandoned me but was still here, present but absent at the same time.

I was torn between missing her so much that my heart felt like it was going to break, to feeling like I could quite happily never see her again.

But tonight, tonight the house felt so big and empty and quiet. I wanted my mom. Here. With me.

I wanted to tell her that I was down, like really low - okay, not as low as I had been at the beginning of the year

- but still, not far off rock-bottom. I wanted her to put her arms around me, to tell me it was alright, that I didn't need the anti-depressant tablets that I was holding, because she would make it go away, she would make it better.

But who was I trying to kid? She couldn't look after herself, let alone me and all my crap. To be honest, she never really had looked after me, not since I was about six, the time my father was diagnosed with cancer. Cancer robbed me of my dad, it also stole my mom.

She couldn't cope. My Gran lived with us anyway, and she watched me whilst Cassie looked after my father, and then, when he died, well, mom's love for me died too. It wasn't so bad then though; it hurt, don't get me wrong, but at least I had Gran to tend to my cuts, to give me magic cream, to go to Parent's Evenings, to look after me when I was sick.

Now I had no one.

I popped an anti-depressant from the foil. A happy pill. If only it was, if only it took it all away. But, I knew it wouldn't. The doctor I'd seen earlier in the evening told me it would sort out the chemical imbalance in my brain, just take the edge off what I was feeling, and make me feel more able to cope with dealing with my problems. He then booked me in to see a Counsellor.

I didn't want a counsellor.

I just wanted to see her, to speak to my mom, really speak like a normal family. But I knew it wouldn't happen, so I went to bed, like she'd told me.

In the morning, the alarm shocked me awake at seven, after another night of unsettled sleep. I could hear clattering downstairs and I remembered Cassie was back. My heart seemed to fall right into the pit of my stomach.

I crawled out of bed and headed for the bathroom. After a quick soak in the shower I grabbed a pair of red jeans and a black top and got dressed before heading downstairs.

I stopped outside the living room door, took a deep breath, making sure I'd glued my fake "I'm okay, everything is totally normal" smile onto my face, before entering. Maybe I should've super-glued it on because, sometimes, it made my jaw physically ache to hold it in place.

'Hi!' I said, as enthusiastically as I could, as I walked through to the kitchen. To my own ears it sounded phoney but it seemed to pass right over her head.

'Oh, hi Hun!' she said, uncurling herself from around a shirtless Dan who frying bacon on the hob. It made me uncomfortable, liked I'd interrupted an intimate moment.

'Hi,' said Dan, looking up from the bacon.

I smiled weakly at him as I was swept up in Cassie's arms.

'I've missed you,' she said, clinging on to me for a few seconds. And another beautiful lie was born. She let me go and held out her hand to reveal a platinum engagement ring with a single heart-shaped diamond. 'Do you like it?'

Diamonds make me feel sick, all that blood spilt for the vanity of others. 'Yes, it's beautiful,' I lied. I couldn't face arguing with her already, not when I'd only just got her back. 'Congratulations!'

'Do you want some breakfast?' asked Dan. 'We've got sausage, bacon, or I could do you some toast?'

'No, it's alright thanks. I'm running late, I'll get some at school.'

'Evelyn, Hun, you need to look after yourself, you're looking tired. Stay, have some breakfast, celebrate with us today,' said Cassie, draping herself around Dan again. 'I can write you a note if you want the day off?'

Cassie's bathrobe had fallen off her shoulder, revealing her newly bronzed skin. She kissed Dan on the neck and I wanted to retch. The thought of staying here, with them. No, I couldn't even think about it.

'No.' I said, quickly adding, 'thanks though. I've got to keep up with my work, A-levels are quite demanding.'

Cassie looked at me for a moment, like she wanted to say something but thought better of it. Finally she said 'Okay, just a thought.'

'Anyway, better go,' I said, grabbing my school bag off the chair, 'or I'll miss my bus.'

'Dan could take you?' said Cassie.

'Nah, it's okay. You two look like you need some alone time.' Shivers of disgust ran down my spine as the words formed in my mouth. I couldn't look at them again, if I did, I thought I might actually be sick. 'See yah!' I said, turning quickly and bolting for the door.

I stepped out into the cold grey morning, unintentionally slamming the front door shut behind me. There was a sprinkling of frost on the floor and the air was cold and crisp, a stark contrast to how stuffy and suffocating it had been in Cassie and Dan's presence.

Cassie. My mom.

Maybe I'd been adopted, or switched at birth.

The idea of Cassie being my mom felt so wrong, so foreign to me, like running naked down the street. We were connected by blood. That was it. But blood doesn't necessarily make family.

The doctor had told me to take a week off, a break from the pressure of studying, but it wasn't the studying that was bothering me. I walked to the bus stop and waited, keeping up the pretence of going to school because I couldn't stay at home, not with them all over each other, but I couldn't go to school, not with the nurse telling me to take the time off too.

The bus journey was uneventful, pulling into Oakwood station just after eight. I stumbled off, swept along in the sea of people hurrying along. They had a purpose, somewhere to be, lives full of families and friends.

I had nothing.

I couldn't go to Sofia's, where I usually went for coffee, as people from school would probably be in there, so I stopped off at Bella's Coffee Shop, and downed a large latte, hoping that the caffeine hit would wake me up. I spent the rest of the day at the library working on assignments or pretending to work as I mainly doodled in my note pad. The hours both dragged and sped by, depending on how I was feeling and what I was doing. It got worse as soon as the clock started ticking towards home-time. I knew I had nowhere else to go; the library would shut soon and I would be forced to go back to them. My stomach churned at the thought, my heart rolled erratically in my chest.

And then I was back home again, sticking on my "Happy" face before I let myself in. There hadn't been any point though, the repetitive banging of a headboard upstairs told me I wouldn't be seeing Cassie and Dan just yet, but I didn't know what was worse; seeing them or hearing what they were up to.

I shuddered. My mind was telling me to run, to get out of there, but where else was I supposed to go?

This was my home. Wasn't it?

I sloped off to the kitchen and flicked on the radio, turning it up loud to drown out their crap. I popped a pod in the coffee machine. At the side of it sat a huge pile of wedding magazines, I closed my eyes and sighed, not sure I had the strength in me to deal with it all.

'Hi Hun, how was your day?' asked Cassie, appearing in the doorway behind me, her lithe body draped in a black silk kimono, her blazing red hair tied up in an untidy ponytail. She still looked gorgeous, like she'd just walked off a Pre-Raphaelite painting with her bright emerald eyes and porcelain skin.

What could I say? Mom, I've got depression. I feel crap. You make me feel like crap. 'Oh, okay. You know. How about you?' I could imagine, and I didn't really want to know.

'It's been,' said Cassie, a dreamy smile on her face, 'really good.'

'Great.' I felt sick inside.

'Yeah, we popped out to get some magazines,' said Cassie pointing to the pile by the coffee machine, 'you'll have to have a flick through so we can see what dress you'd like. There are some gorgeous ones.'

'A dress?'

'Of course. Do you think I wouldn't have my only daughter as a bridesmaid? Was thinking of asking Celia too, what d'ya think?'

'It's your day,' I said, grabbing my coffee tightly in one hand whilst piling loads of sugar into it with the other.

'Yeah, I think Celia would like that. Oh, by the way, Celia's invited us over tonight for dinner so you'll have to make your own tea. Is that ok?'

I nodded. What did she want? Permission? As if she'd change her plans for me anyway. 'Yeah, I've got to go to Sam's in a minute anyway. We're working on an art assignment together, so I've already arranged to eat with him,' I lied. Why was it so easy to lie to my own mother?

'Okay Hun,' said Cassie. She swept over to me and took a handful of my hair. It made me cringe as she ran her fingers through it. 'We'll have to do something with your hair.' No one had touched my hair like that, not since my Gran had died. I instinctively pulled away from her touch. She didn't even notice. 'Oh, there's a pressie there for you, hope you like it.' She pointed to a small pink gift bag on the counter.

I picked it up and fetched out the gift; a bottle of Opium perfume (I hate strong perfumes), some face cream (I never use the stuff) and a Chick-lit novel, called Dreaming of You, the yellow price sticker still stuck on its cover (a bargain at two pounds). 'Thanks,' I said carefully putting them back into the bag. I'd stuff the face cream and perfume in the bathroom cupboard (with the other unopened bottles) later, and find a space on the bookshelf for the book, next to all the other un-read novels she'd bought me (all Chick-lit, which she knew I couldn't stand. I didn't believe in love).

Her gifts only served to show me how far apart we had drifted, a reminder of how little she knew me. Or how little she wanted to know me.

I was a complete alien to my mother; in the same room, but so many worlds apart.

'I only came back for my art folder, so I better go else I'm going to be late,' I said, leaving my gift bag and untouched coffee on the counter.

I headed upstairs and bumped into Dan coming out of the bathroom, wearing nothing but a towel around his waist, low enough to show the scar from where he'd had his appendix removed.

'Hi,' he said, standing in the doorway, brushing his hair away from his face like he was some sort of Adonis.

'Hi,' I replied, looking away. My skin was crawling like a whole colony of ants were scuttling over me, burrowing into my skin. Why couldn't they just leave me alone? Why did they have to make me feel so uncomfortable in my own home?

I dived into my room and grabbed my art folder, before racing downstairs and fleeing the house. 'See ya!' I shouted, to no one in particular.

Outside, darkness was beginning to tumble down like leaves in the autumn and frost was smearing his sticky white fingers over every surface. And I was cold, alone, and miserable.

I'd got nowhere to go, so I just walked, and walked, until I knew it would be safe to go back home.

The house was shrouded in darkness when I finally returned. I ran upstairs for a shower but found Dan's clothes all over the floor like an infestation of parasites. I gave up and went to bed to read, only to be disturbed again by Cassie and Dan stumbling back in late. Soon after the headboard started banging. I shut out the noise with music on my headphones.

I don't know at what time I managed to fall to sleep, but when I finally did drift off I had a strange dream; a figure emerged from the depths of my mind, taking my hand firmly in theirs and sweeping me up into their arms. I couldn't see their face and yet I knew it was a man, I could feel it in my heart as his cold hands grasped me tightly. My body stirred under his touch and then, when I felt the touch of his cold lips on mine, my whole body came to light, as if a fire had ignited inside me. My whole body ached for him, wanted to be part of him. I wanted to stay there forever, locked in his embrace.

My eyes flew open, a thump, thump, thump of a headboard on the bedroom wall brought me right back to harsh reality.

My first dream in what had seemed like an eternity, and they had to go and spoil it. I mean, how old was Cassie anyway? Did they really have to be at it like rabbits?

I lay in my bed, clasping my stomach, trying to hold onto the feeling that had burned so brightly inside me in my dream. I wanted the feeling back, so I closed my eyes and tried hard to remember every detail, tried to piece together the fragments that were left in my head. But it was no good, the banging of the bed beat the thoughts from my head.

I had to get out of the house, I couldn't stand it.

I bounced out of bed and clutched angrily at a pile of clothes on the floor. How dare they come back and take the one place that I felt like I could be myself! It was bloody unfair of them, I thought -pulling on the first woollen jumper I came to - that they had stolen my one sanctuary.

I dived into the bathroom, washed my face, brushed my teeth, and quickly pulled a brush through my hair. Then, I left the house.

Outside it was still dark, the street lamps still lighting up the sky with their sickly orange glow. I wrapped my arms around myself to keep warm and began walking.

Now and then, I bumped into people who said hello but I ignored them; I was in too foul a mood to deal with their happy lives. There was a family coming out of a house on Cope street, a little girl with curly blonde hair and her blue eyed older brother laughing despite the cold and earliness of the hour. They grasped their mother's hand as she led them to her car. Their mother was smiling as the little girl was telling her about having to wave at the trees because they were waving at her.

I looked away, jealous of their happiness.

Evie

A week of pretending to be at school, faking that I was happy, that I was normal, was exhausting. I was glad when Monday arrived and I was back at school. I went out early, stopping off at Sofia's for a coffee to give me some sort of Dutch courage or something. I could feel my heart racing away with itself in my chest, my palms were sweaty and I was in danger of anxiety overload.

I switched my phone on. I hadn't done that for over a week; there seemed no point when no one really wanted to talk to me. A pang of loneliness slithered across my insides.

I scrolled down the list of text messages that had built up since it had been off; there were many from the same people who had been trolling my e-mail account; Ali57 and Razorgirl. I didn't even bother to open them; I didn't want to pick open my wounds today. Besides, as much as they cut me in two when I read them, even I had to admit that they lacked originality. "Die Bitch" seemed to be their particular favourite at the moment.

I deleted them.

Then there was a string of messages from Sam, all saying pretty much the same thing; "Are you ok?", "Haven't seen you for a while?", "Do you want me to come over?", "You're quiet?", "Why are you ignoring me?", "Fine, I won't bother". And then nothing since the last one, dated three days ago.

A new message flashed up from Cassie; "Are you ok?" Do you really expect me to reply? I thought to myself. Do you really want to know? No. Of course you don't. So stop pretending!

The message continued: "You left early today, I wanted to ask you something, come home straight after school and I'll ask you then, Mom xxx."

I deleted that too.

I pressed on Sam's number. After a few rings he picked up.

'Hello.' His voice was lacking its usual warmth.

'Hey, you ok?' I asked, trying to sound casual, like a gulf hadn't opened up between us.

'Yeah, why are you ringing me now?'

'Oh Sam, I'm sorry I didn't get back to you. I've been really ill and my phone's been playing up, the battery or something-'

'All week?'

I bit my lip. I could taste the metallic flavour of blood. It was so unlike him to be even a little bit angry with me. 'I know, I'm sorry. Life's been....life's been crap; Cassie's got engaged-'

'Again?' asked Sam, his voice rising a few octaves.

'Yep.'

'Do you want to tell me about it over breakfast?'

I felt myself relax. 'I'm already at Sofia's.'

'Okay, give me ten and I'll be there.'

The phone went dead and I was all alone again. Claire, the waitress, came over and placed my coffee and toast in front of me. I said thank you and cupped my hands around the steaming mug of coffee, watching the steam spiral up into the air.

The growing chasm of loneliness was opening up inside of me, bubbling and churning, trying to swallow me whole. I pushed my toast away; I just couldn't face it.

I grabbed my tablets from my bag, popped one in my mouth and took a long sip of coffee. The coffee burned my throat as it travelled down. I hoped it would burn the feeling of loneliness away too. But it didn't.

After ten minutes, Sam strolled into the cafe, the biggest smile on his face. Dependable, loyal Sam. I didn't deserve him.

We'd been boyfriend and girlfriend in year eight. It'd lasted two months and we'd never got passed the hand-holding stage. He'd told me his deepest darkest secret; that he preferred boys to girls. I didn't care; I'd got secrets of my own. It was these secrets that had bonded us in the beginning and had held us together as we'd grown. Until recently.

Now we seemed to be sailing away from each other. Ships travelling in opposite directions.

'Hello!' he said, sliding into the chair next to me, his face shining with his same goofy smile. But things weren't the same. We'd changed.

There was a time when that smile would've made me feel a million times better, but it had been so long now since his words or smile could comfort me. Maybe it was me that had changed, or I had stagnated as the world moved on.

But I still loved him, like he was my own brother.

'Hiya,' I said, 'how are you?'

'I'm fine but God, you look like shit!' he said, smiling widely again.

'Thanks.'

'My pleasure,' he said, pulling the plate of cold toast over to him, 'Do you mind?'

I shook my head. 'No, go ahead,' I said, rolling my eyes, 'I'm sure that's all you hang around with me for!'

'Well, it's not your good looks, is it?'

I smacked his shoulder with my hand.

'Anyway, you owe me, not answering my messages. I was worried, you know after...'But Sam let the sentence hang and took another big bite of toast.

Immediately the atmosphere changed; a black cloud had entered the room and I knew that Sam felt that way too. Maybe that was what had come between us, my inability to share with Sam how low I'd fallen. Why did I treat him like this?

'No, I'm okay.' I looked at his face; he didn't believe me. 'Honestly,' I said, 'It's just Cassie, getting engaged again.'

'Another engagement, eh?'

'Yep, she's asked me to be bridesmaid-'

'Eugh!' said Sam, exaggerating a shudder, 'imagining you in a posh dress is turning me off your toast!'

'Thanks. It's been hell living with her since she got back, you should try living with it.'

'No, thanks. Got enough with my own parents.'

Guilt suddenly ripped through me. I could feel my shame written in red over my face. How could I be so ignorant of my best friend's life? 'Is everything okay?'

'Yeah, yeah,' he said, with a light dismissal of the hand, 'nothing I can't handle.'

So, he didn't trust me enough to tell me. Had I really let him down that bad?

'So, what was wrong with you last week?'

'Just the flu,' I lied, as Sam pretended to recoil in horror, 'I'm okay now though!' We were both keeping things from each other. But what else was I supposed to say? Oh, yeah, sorry Sam, I wasn't at school because I'm depressed? 'So, what've I missed?' I asked, trying to divert the conversation before the tears, building at the back of my throat, exploded. I was struggling, despite my promise not to cry in front of people. I didn't know what was wrong with me; I usually had no problem locking them inside of me, until recently.

'Loads,' he said, but then he saw the look of horror on my face and added, 'nothing you can't catch up with though!'

'Great!' I said, leaning back in my chair. I pulled at the collar of my jumper; I was starting to feel really hot and an uncomfortable sicky feeling was building in the pit of my stomach.

'Are you okay? Are you sure you're over-'

'I'm fine,' I lied, again, putting my hand in the air to stop any more questions. I realised my legs were bouncing up and down under the table.

'Don't worry,' he said, putting his hand on my shoulder. 'It's only the beginning of A-levels, you'll make up what you've missed, easy. You'll cinch it.'

I smiled weakly.

'Come on, let's go before we're late.'

I nodded, scraping back my chair. I stood up and grabbed my bag, but my head started swimming. My legs felt like lead, and they didn't want to move, they wanted to melt away so they didn't have to hold me up. The fluttering was starting in my chest again and I felt really, really hot.

'Are you sure you're okay?' asked Sam.

'Yeah, must still be a little flu-y, I'll be fine,' I replied, steadying myself with a hand on the table.

'Come here,' said Sam, placing his arm around me.

It felt good to have his arm around me, to have someone there to support me. He smelt of soap and hair mousse and comfort and warmth, and friendship. How had I let him slip so far away?

He held me all the way to school. It really was a good thing he was there because I don't know whether I would've made it to school otherwise. My legs seemed to have developed a mind of their own and they really didn't want to work. Being with Sam forced me to move, forced me to keep going forwards, to not turn around and run away.

As we passed through the cafeteria I heard Amber say at the top of her voice, 'Ah, look, they've let the freaks out on day release.'

I tried to ignore her, tried to hold my head up high. It was a struggle as my insides felt like they were crumbling in on themselves, but I was determined that I wouldn't let her make me run. I was not going to run.

The first day back was so hard. I saw the nurse and she took notes, telling me that she would have to inform the teachers. I agreed, adding, 'Please don't tell my mom.' I didn't need that, not at the moment. All I could imagine was that this would come out, Cassie and Dan would argue and then split and it would all be my fault; everything else was my fault. I couldn't deal with that. The nurse wasn't impressed, but agreed as long as I kept going to see her.

When I got home that afternoon, I was relieved to not be greeted by the sound of a banging headboard, but that relief was short-lived as I found Cassie and Celia hunched over the dining table, surrounded by swatches of fabric and piles of open wedding magazines full of expensive cakes, dresses and bouquets.

'I think,' said Celia, pulling a magazine to her, 'that's gorgeous. This dress would look so good on you. That dress with a crimson rose bouquet would be amazing for a winter wedding.'

'You know, that would be so romantic. Christmas Eve would be lovely wouldn't it? Especially if we could book Saint John's.'

I cringed when Cassie said Saint John's, it just seemed so disrespectful and such a repugnant idea. Dad is buried there, I wanted to say, you married *him* there, but all I managed was 'Hello.'

Cassie looked up, her green eyes dazzling like emeralds. It was easy to see why men were so captivated by her. 'Hi Hun, you had a good day?'

'Yeah, thanks,' I said, sidling on past them and into the kitchen.

'Come and have a look at what Celia and I have been doing,' she shouted after me.

I closed my eyes and took a deep breath before answering. 'Okay, let me get a glass of water first.' I heard Celia mutter something, but I couldn't quite make out what it was. I grabbed a drink and then went back into the dining room. 'So, what've you been up to?' I asked, trying to muster as much enthusiasm as I could.

'We've been swimming,' said Celia.

'Really, I didn't think you could swim-'

'Der!' said Celia, sneering at me, her horsey mouth contorted like she was about to neigh, 'Of course we haven't been swimming. We've been looking at wedding stuff.' She said the last words really slowly like I was hard of hearing, but then, I had just walked straight into it.

'Right,' I said.

'Yeah, look at this,' said Cassie, pushing a magazine over to me. It was a picture of a stick thin model dressed in an ivory taffeta gown.

'That's nice.'

'Nice? What kind of word is "nice"?' asked Celia.

'That's better,' I said, sitting down and pulling another magazine towards me. I was not going to let Celia get the better of me. Not this time. 'That would really suit you, Mom.' I presented the open magazine to Cassie, it had a picture of a model in a simple vintage silk dress. 'Simple and yet elegant. You'd look like a movie star.'

Cassie's eyes widened as she took the magazine to get a better look at the dress, 'I love it!'

'You'd look like Ava Gardner or Rita Hayworth,' I said, adding the last name in hope of a response. My dad loved the old black and white movies, especially Rita Hayworth in Gilda.

'That would be a great theme,' said Cassie, putting the magazine on the table, so that she could spread her hands in the air, 'The Golden Age of Hollywood.'

'A theme? That's a bit last Century, isn't it?' said Celia, her face looked like she was sucking a lemon. Not much different to normal.

'Oh Celia, come on, it'd be fun!' said Cassie, placing her head playfully on Celia's shoulder. 'No,' she said, raising her head from Celia's shoulder, her eyes brimming with excitement, 'even better, what about fancy dress at the party?'

'A party?' I asked. My voice sounded like I'd sucked the helium out of a ten balloons, it was that high.

'Yeah, next Friday,' said Cassie, looking up at me through her eyelashes, her head tilted to the side, 'it's Celia's present to me and Dan, an engagement party at the club where Carl works. You up for it?'

'Yeah,' I said, trying to sound really excited. I wasn't. But what else could I say? I could feel Celia's eyes boring down on me. I didn't look at her.

'What about an Eighties and Nineties disco-'

'Really?' asked Celia.

'Yeah, come on Sis, let's dance like we used to! Let's forget all the bad stuff and just dance!' Cassie looked at Celia with her pleading "lost puppy" face. 'Come on, it'll be fun!'

'And fancy dress?' asked Celia.

Cassie didn't say a word, but her face lit up with a huge smile and I knew Celia didn't stand a chance.

'Okay,' said Celia, finally cracking a smile, 'It'll be fun, I'll sort it with Tom the DJ and I'll text or e-mail everyone to say it's fancy dress.'

'Thank you!' said Cassie, flinging her arms around her sister.

This week was now feeling more like a war zone - my first counselling session, a fancy dress party, and somehow I had to pin down Dexter, to arrange a time to work on our English presentation, due in first Monday after the holiday, even though he was one of the last people I really wanted to talk to right at that moment, but time was ticking and I couldn't afford to fail English.

How the hell was I going to get through it all?

Evie

The demonic beast inside me was growing fat, feeding on my fears and anxieties that I dragged around like a ball and chain. The idea of the engagement party was filling me with horror, and every day as it drew closer, I could feel the dark cloud above me growing stronger. Even worse, Celia had told me not to worry about the costume for the party because she'd sort it out, but as Celia hated me, I knew I should do the complete opposite and worry like Hell. Celia was never nice, not to me. But before I even got to the party, I had counselling to get through and, more worryingly, I had to try and sort out study time with Dexter for our mixed pairs English presentation, because he didn't look like he was going to make the first move and we only had a few weeks left before the half-term holiday.

We were back in our usual seats for English (we were supposed to be working on the presentations in our own time which was proving a little bit difficult). We had English together on Tuesday afternoon so I decided I'd grab him then, at the end of class. I didn't want to, and the thought of speaking to him actually made me feel sick, but

I couldn't fail English, I didn't need any more crap in my life.

When the bell went for end of school, Mrs Jones dismissed us, but before Dexter could run off I was ready. I leapt out of my seat at the back of the class and bounded over to where he sat with Amber.

'Er...Dexter?' I said. He looked up and I could feel myself blushing. Amber sneered at me from under her thick lashes. Suddenly I felt very hot. I pulled at the neck of my jumper, feeling as though the eyes of the world were watching me, not just Dexter, Amber or any of the sixth formers still loitering in the class. 'We need to work out a time to work on the presentation, I was thinking, we could do it in our free period, tomorrow-'

'He's busy,' said Amber, quickly jumping in, her arm sliding across Dexter's shoulder.

'Well, we need to sort it out,' I said, focusing on Dexter, on being strong and just standing on the spot rather than running away, which is what my legs really wanted to do. I just kept telling myself that I couldn't fail, I had to get this presentation done, one way or another, even if it killed me. 'It needs to be done by the Monday after half-term, and I can't do it over half-term-'

'Like I said, he's busy.'

Dexter huffed. He stuffed his paper and books into his bag.

'I was speaking to Dexter, not you,' I said, sounding a little bit angrier than I had intended. I just wanted to get the goddamn assignment done. I didn't need this, I'd got too many things going on in my life and I could feel it all churning around in my stomach. 'After all, it's Dexter that I'm doing the presentation with, not you.'

Amber's mouth dropped open and she stared at me with incredulous eyes. She looked like she was trying to find something nasty to say. 'Dexter,' she said, finally, but the venom in her voice was purely for my benefit.

Dexter stood up quickly and grabbed his bag off the table. Amber's face fell as he let her arm fall away roughly from his shoulders. He rummaged around in his bag before fetching out a wodge of folded, dog-eared, paper. 'Here,' he said, thrusting it into my chest. 'It's all my stuff for the presentation, you can work around it.' He brushed passed me, leaving Amber sitting alone at the table.

'But we're supposed to be working on this together,' I called after him. 'How are we going to pass if we don't-'

He stopped abruptly in the middle of the room, and spun on the spot to face me. 'Yeah, well, that's not my problem. I tried to get us new partners but Mrs Jones isn't having any of it. I might have to work with you in class, but that doesn't mean I want to spend time with you outside of it, does it?'

'But-'

'God, Evelyn will you just look at yourself! When will you stop it?' He strode back across the room, closing the distance between us quickly. I was suddenly aware that the room had fallen deathly quiet. People were circling around us, like a baying mob waiting for the violence they knew was coming.

'I-' I didn't know what to say. I felt like a fox caught in the middle of a pack of hunting dogs. What little strength I had, (that had kept me in front of him, that had kept me together despite wanting to run) was now vanishing. Tears were building at the back of my throat, but I couldn't let them see me cry. I was losing my grip, teetering on the edge. I tried to hold my breath hoping that by doing so, it would prevent Dexter from exploding in front of me as I knew he was going to, that it would stop him from saying those things that I didn't want to hear.

'You're embarrassing. You've been following me around like a lost puppy for months-'

'But-'

'And you're getting worse, staring at me in class-'

'I don't-'

'Whatever, Evelyn. It's pathetic. You're pathetic, and I've had enough!'

'I'm-' I wanted to fight back, tell him I wasn't, but words we're failing me.

'You seem to think,' he said, his eyes blazing with a dark and troubling fury, 'for some reason that I'd be interested in a skank like you. You're just a tart like your mother. I mean, how many is that she's been with now? She's like the town bike.' There were giggles. Amber came to stand by him, looking like the cat who'd just got the cream. Or the bitch that had the dog.

'Thanks,' I said. But those words were like oxygen to a piece of tinder, and ignited some fire hidden deep within me. A fire that I'd forgotten I had. Fiery anger arose from nowhere, springing out of me like a coil. 'If I'm such a skank, why the Hell did you save me?' My anger momentarily surprised him. I'd surprised myself. Maybe after my tears, anger was all that was left.

'Save you?' he asked, his face scrunched up as he tried to dismiss what I'd said, 'I didn't save you!'

'So you didn't pull me out of the water on New year's Eve?' I knew everyone was listening, I knew I'd said too much, but what the Hell, I couldn't take it back now. And even if I could, what would be the point?

'No,' he said, his face relaxing as if it all now made sense to him. 'I didn't save you. You were lying on the towpath, out of your head.'

'But-'

'You were lying on the towpath, drunk. A pisshead like your mother.'

I glared and pointed my finger at him, not believing a word he said. 'So how did I get home? Why was your earring in my room?'

'You opened your eyes, slurred something about going home, so we took you home, despite the fact that you stank. We dragged you home, you took yourself upstairs to bed. We needed somewhere to hang so we stayed there-'

'Your earring?'

'Hell, Evie, what do you want me to say? It probably dropped off when I was dragging you home! When are you going to get it through your thick pisshead brain of yours that you mean nothing to me?'

I exhaled loudly as I finally understood. So I meant nothing to him. It hadn't even crossed his mind that I might've tried to kill myself. He thought I was just drunk.

'Hey,' said Sam, appearing at my side, out of nowhere.

'But you saved me,' I said, stepping forward, searching his face for something. Anything.

'Don't be stupid,' he said, taking a step backwards, 'I could never be with someone like you, so don't be getting that Stockholm Syndrome or whatever it is because I'm not interested.'

'That's enough,' said Sam, stepping in between me and Dexter.

'You heard what he said,' said Amber. She was loving every minute of it.

Sam turned to me. 'Come on, grab your stuff, I'll walk you out.'

I looked up, into Sam's deep blue eyes, and felt them cut me in two as he searched my face for answers. I didn't speak, but turned and grabbed my stuff off the table.

We walked to the school gates in silence. Sam had his arm around me, protecting me, but I could feel the sorrow weighing him down.

He let his arm drop from my shoulders and reluctantly I turned to face him.

'So,' he said, 'what was all that about?'

His face was ashen, the hurt visible in the way he looked at me, and in the tone of his voice.

'Nothing.' I didn't want to talk about it. Any of it. I was too full of anger, too ashamed, and I didn't want to hurt him anymore.

'Don't lie to me.'

I sighed. No, I shouldn't be lying to you. I cleared my throat, feeling the drizzle soaking me to the bone. In the distance, the sun's rays had managed to poke through the cloud. A small rainbow curved in the sky, like a great stone arch in God's natural cathedral. 'Those photos you asked me about-'

'I knew it! You did, didn't you? You tried to ki-'

'No!' I had to stop him, even if that meant more lies. I couldn't hear those words fall from his mouth. 'No,' I repeated.

'Don't-'

I put my hand on his arm. 'Sam, I didn't.' Luckily Dexter had given me the perfect, ready-made excuse. 'I'd had too much to drink, tried to walk home,' I said, watching the emotions flick over his face; relief, anger, sadness, 'and ended up falling in the river. I stupidly thought Dexter had saved me.'

'Oh Ev, how stupid can you get?'

'I know, I know,' I said, grabbing onto his arm tighter. Why? Why was I lying? How had everything gone so wrong? 'I didn't tell you the truth because I knew you'd react like this. I didn't want to hurt you.'

'But you have, by not telling me. Why didn't you just tell me when I asked you before?'

I shrugged. 'I know. I'm sorry, I felt so ashamed that...' I couldn't take it anymore. I flung my arms around him and he held on to me tightly. 'Sam, I really am sorry,' I said, buried deep in his warmth.

'Just promise me you'll tell me next time, if something happens.'

'I promise,' I said, but the lies were proving too much, they were lying heavy on my heart. My heart broke and I started to sob.

Sam held on to me. It felt so good. And yet so bad.

'Oh Ev, when did it get this bad?'

I couldn't reply. If I had, I think that the truth would have forced itself out of my mouth and then there would've been no going back.

The next day at school Sam hovered over me like a protective father. I kind of appreciated it (he was only trying to look out for me), but after History together and him waiting for me outside the toilets every time I went in, even interrogating me if I spent too long in there (so weird, it was just plain wrong), I felt really claustrophobic. I had to get away.

I told him I had to go home in my free lesson now, that I couldn't have met Dexter anyway as Cassie and Celia were having a girly meeting about the wedding, that I had to go because, if I didn't, I would suffer in the long run. He'd looked at me, searching my eyes for any tell-tale signs that I was lying, but he didn't find any. I was getting far too good at it. To my shame.

Thankfully, when I did get home, Cassie and Dan were out, so I grabbed a coffee and shut myself in my room, knowing that way, at least for a while, I wouldn't have to speak to them if they came back. I spent the rest of the afternoon reading through Dexter's hastily written notes, trying to decipher his writing, before researching my part and merging the two together. If he didn't want to work with me, fine, he'd just have to read out what I'd written wouldn't he?

But guilt kept slapping me in the face as I kept thinking about my little lies to Sam, after all he was only trying to be a good friend. I hadn't even told him about the counselling session I'd got the next day.

I decided I'd text him in the morning, tell him I had to go to the doctors or something. Maybe I should've made it up to him by inviting him to the party on Friday night, but I wasn't sure I was ready for that. I didn't know if I wanted the two sides of my life to merge like that. I liked it the way it was; separate, at least then I could control what each side knew about me. Besides, it was going to be hell anyway, so why would I put Sam through that when I could bear it on my own?

I stood outside the counselling building, the next morning, and texted Sam. I told him that I was okay, but I'd be in later because I'd had to go to the doctors so, hopefully, he wouldn't worry about me being missing. It was still grey outside; the drizzle had given way to showers, and people hurried by, hunched under their umbrellas. I watched, from under the porch, as a sharp gust of wind stole a Batman umbrella off a small boy. It rolled down the street like tumble weed in an old western.

From outside, the counselling building looked like an average detached house. It was only the blue and white plaque for OCS, Oakwood Counselling Services, and the posters for pregnancy help and crisis services that distinguished it from any other house in the tree-lined suburban street. I pressed the doorbell and waited, my hood over my face in case anyone saw me.

A woman with a grey bob and glasses perched high on her head, opened the front door.

'Hi,' she said, 'can I help you?'

'Yes, I've got an appointment at nine,' I said.

'What's the name?'

'Evelyn, Evelyn Anderson.'

'Oh, hi Evelyn,' she said, stepping forward with her hand extended in greeting, 'Pleased to meet you.'

I took her hand, but her handshake was loose.

'Please come in and take a seat, I'll be with you in a short while.'

I followed her inside and took a seat in the waiting room. The room was bright with a big bay window that flooded the room with light even on such a grey morning, but a dark feeling hung in the air, in the ripped wallpaper and the dog-eared posters. On the coffee table in the middle of the room, women's magazines were piled up, dating from about two centuries ago, but still spewing out the same old crap; "How Karina lost two dress sizes in a week", "Suzy shows her cellulite on boozy girls' holiday", some footballer's wife called Tallulah had had her breasts enlarged and someone called Alex had been caught having an affair.

I removed my hood and started fiddling with the strap on my bag, my legs bouncing up and down of their own accord. I wanted to run. I felt dirty. Like I had a dirty little secret. Well, I did have a dirty little secret didn't I?

'Evelyn Anderson?' said the same woman who'd let me in, 'if you'd like to follow me? I'm ready for you now.'

The woman took me down a corridor and into a smaller room at the back of the house. It had two red leather sofas sat facing each other like a pair of lips, a small wooden coffee table in the middle like a misshapen tongue, and in the corner of the room sat a small desk piled high with files and a computer that looked like it belonged in the Prehistoric era.

'Please sit down Evelyn,' said the woman, pointing at the farthest sofa.

I sat down, clutching my bag on my lap.

The woman put a box of tissues beside me before perching on the end of the opposite sofa. That didn't fill me with confidence.

'Hi Evelyn,' she said, reaching out, over the coffee table, to shake my hand again.

I took it. It was cold, her hold still insubstantial. My Gran always told me not to trust people with loose handshakes. 'Hi,' I said, more to the floor.

'My names Grace Harlow,' she said, taking her glasses off her head and placing them over her eyes, 'and I'm your counsellor. So, I see you've been referred here by the GP?'

I nodded.

She picked up the cardboard file next to her on the sofa and opened it, quickly scanning over it with her eyes. 'Okay, so let me just confirm your address?'

A file. A handful of paper, pieces of my life. 'Thirty-three Oakwood Road.'

'Okay, date of birth?'

'Seventh of November, nineteen-ninety-five.'

Grace Harlow shut the file and looked at me, from over the top of her glasses. Her eyes were grey, like the weather outside. 'So, this is a session led by you. You can use this forty-five minutes to talk about whatever you like, whatever's bothering you or getting you down. If you want to rant at me that's also fine, okay?' she asked, tilting her head in a show of empathy.

But her empathy was lost on me in the cold and drab space. Why would I talk to her? Why would I spew my guts out to a stranger?

She adjusted the red cardigan draped over her shoulders and leaned back in the chair, waiting for me to speak.

But I couldn't.

My words wouldn't leave me, they were mine, and mine alone. I didn't trust her with them.

'I know this is hard,' she said, after a few minutes of silence, 'and it's perfectly okay if you just want this time to sit and think and be quiet, but it can be really helpful to talk about things.'

Still I couldn't speak. I didn't trust her, in her flowery blouse with her loose handshake.

She crossed her legs. 'So, you've been feeling depressed?'

I nodded.

'How long have you been on the tablets now?'

'About two weeks.'

'And are they starting to work would you say? Are you feeling any better?'

No. I feel like everything is too loud. 'Yes.'

'Well that's a good start. The tablets won't take it away, but they'll take the edge off, allow you to try and tackle the root issues behind the depression.'

I nodded.

Grace Harlow un-crossed her legs. 'What about inviting your mother to the next session? Sometimes-'

'No,' I said, a little too forcefully. Damn. I'd given her more information than I had wanted to.

Grace Harlow tilted her head again and looked at me. I turned away.

'Do you get on with your mother?'

I shook my head. Grace sat there, waiting for my confessions to come tumbling out. But they didn't.

'What about your dad?'

'He's dead.'

'Oh. Okay, so how do you feel about that?'

No. I didn't trust her. I wasn't going to say anymore. This stuff was off-limits.

'Do you miss your father?'

I sat still as stone. Still off-limits.

'Do you have any friends, anyone else you can talk to?'

Off-limits.

'What about Grandparents?'

No. I didn't want to tell her anything. The stranger with a grey bob and flowery blouse. Why was I even here? It wasn't like anyone was making me come here. I stood up. 'Sorry, I can't do this.'

'That's okay. I told you, you don't have to tell me anything-'

'I've got to go...too stuffy in here.'

'Okay, take my card,' said Grace standing up, holding out her business card, 'ring me when you've evened out a bit more. At any time, whenever you need to talk.'

I took the card and fled from the nondescript house, feeling more empowered than I ever had. I would talk when I wanted to.

Josh

I'd been wallowing in self-pity for days, not daring to leave the apartment in case I was tempted to follow Evie again. I had to stay away, for my own sake as well as hers. What had I been thinking, trying to get her to see me?

Staying inside my prison, waiting for Death to summon me again, was preferable to that torture. I could feel the axe swinging ever closer to my neck, the release of death not far away. I would just wait it out until She'd decided I'd served my purpose.

And that would be sooner, rather than later, because without Evie, what was the point? I wasn't going to do anything else for Death, I would refuse her and She would have to finish me.

Death didn't know me. She never had.

I was lying on my bed, drowning my sorrows with another bottle of absinthe. There was something about the green liquid that spoke to me like an old friend, promising me that I would forget my troubles.

But it's honeyed tongue had lied to me.

It hadn't worked.

My misery still clasped onto my ankles and wouldn't let go, despite how much I drank. Instead, it felt as though the absinthe was nourishing my troubles, helping them to grow stronger and more alive with every mouthful.

At some point I fell asleep, the drink letting my mind to wander into its darkest recesses, allowing me to dream.

I was lying half dead in a ditch, maggots crawling across my skin, eating me alive. A ripe full moon hung in the sky above me, obscured now and again by curtains of clouds that shut out the light, leaving me in complete darkness for minutes at a time. I was terrified of the dark, of the not knowing what was out there in the shadows, lurking with the wolves that howled and whined. I felt something wriggling around in my cheek. I reached up to touch, my arm half-eaten and bloodied. I screamed, a scream that seemed to last for an eternity - a scream so loud that it probably could've been heard in Hell - and my face exploded. A black fly burst from my cheek, and extended its silvery wings to fly.

I woke up, drenched in sweat, I could feel the damp bed sheets clinging to my back. Slowly I opened my eyes and shuddered in terror; Death was sitting next to me on the bed, her pale hand resting on my cheek.

She sighed, 'Oh, Josh.'

I shunted the empty absinthe bottle off my chest and onto the other side of the bed. 'What do you want?' I asked, pulling myself up into a sitting position.

Death ran her tongue over her blood red lips, and She let her hand fall onto my naked chest, 'You're a clever boy, you work it out.'

I pulled the white sheet up to my abdomen to cover my nakedness. She looked like She wanted to eat me. 'What if I don't want to?'

'Or maybe you're not as clever as I thought,' She said, her jaw clenching.

'Why don't you just leave me alone? I've had enough, just get it over with because I'm not doing whatever it is you want me to do. I'm out.' I grabbed the sheet in my hand and jumped off the other side of the bed. I quickly found some jeans and pulled them on. 'I'm done.'

'You still haven't grasped how this works, have you?'

I turned around to bite back, but She was standing right in front of me, taking me off guard.

'You don't get to decide when it's over, my love,' She said, cupping my chin in Her hand.

'I'm not doing it,' I said, staring straight into the black pools of her eyes.

'Ah, is baby throwing a tantrum because he can't get what he wants?'

'I'm done. I want to die, just get it over with.'

Death laughed in my face. 'And that is definitely not something that you get to decide.' She removed Her hand from my chin, letting her fingers wander down my neck and onto my shoulders.

Suddenly She was at the back of me, Her one arm around my neck, a fistful of my hair wrapped tightly in her other hand. 'How would you like to go?' She whispered into my ear, pulling my head to the side. 'Quickly? I could snap your neck in a second. No?'

I remained still, my mind still woozy from the alcohol.

She let my hair go. 'Or, I could run you through with this.' From out of nowhere, She had my angelic dagger, Heaven's Will (that I use to sever the souls of the dead from their bodies) at my throat. 'But if I did that, I would make sure you died a slow and painful death, forcing you to watch as the blood drips away from you, drop by drop, with your life.'

'Do it!' I said, jabbing my neck into the tip of the knife. I felt a trickle of warm blood dribbling down my skin.

She pulled the knife away from my throat and ran her tongue over my bloodied neck. She threw me forward, and I fell heavily to my knees, pain erupting through me as my wings burst from my back. Death grabbed my head and pushed me hard on to the floor. I was unable to move as She climbed on top of me, hissing like some feral cat. She sat astride me, as if I were a dragon, or a griffin, She were taking for a ride.

'The way I'd prefer to do it,' She said, leaning forward, and spitting the words into my ear, 'is by plucking these wings straight from your back.'

She clamped her hands onto either wing, digging her sharp claws into them and yanking them brutally in the wrong direction. My mind flashed back to the first time She had plucked my wings; terror uncoiled within me, but I would not let Her see it.

'DO IT!' I screamed, 'I WANT TO DIE!'

The pain immediately disappeared, along with my wings, and the air stilled, like nothing had ever happened. And yet, I knew it had, because I could feel the memory of it haunting my insides.

Death remained on my back. I could hear her panting hard, trying to regain control, desperate to restrain her anger. After a few moments of silence, She dismounted. 'Get up!' She ordered.

I didn't move. I couldn't move. I lay prostrate on the ground, praying for death.

She grabbed a handful of my hair and hoisted me off the floor. Once I was on my feet, She spun me around to face Her.

'You owe me,' She said, closing her cold hand around my neck.

'Go on then,' I spat. 'Do it.' My near-death experience was making me bold. Or stupid.

'I will tell you when it is time to die, and now is not that time. I wonder,' She said, tightening her grip around my neck ever so slightly, 'what Evie would look like with my hand around her throat?'

I stared back at her black eyes. Black like Her soul. 'You.' But I stopped, knowing the answer to my unspoken question. My shoulders slackened automatically, the fight in me simply vanished. Of course She would do it.

'I see you're finally ready to co-operate. Go and clean yourself up, we need to talk.'

Ten minutes later, I'd cleaned myself up and was sitting on the couch next to Death, watching Her cold hands clasping a coffee mug and imagining Her hands around Evie's neck.

She took a sip of coffee. 'That's disgusting,' she said, pulling a face as She put the mug down on the table, 'You really can't make coffee.'

I stared at the stain of red lipstick left on the mug.

She looked at me like a parent telling off a small child. 'I really can't believe you made me do that. I will pretend,' She said, running her hands over her bright red skirt to brush out the creases, 'that that earlier nonsense didn't happen, but don't ever do that to me again, do you hear?'

I nodded, not really listening.

'Anyway, to business. I need you to pay Obadiah another visit. It seems Hyperion plans to go much further than just cleaving his angelic music.'

I couldn't concentrate on what She was saying, I just kept watching Her blood-red lips moving, as I tried to tune out Her voice.

'I think he's trying to re-unite the Apocalyptic Relics.'

What? Those words grabbed my attention. 'The Apocalyptic Relics?' I said, tearing my gaze away from her lips, 'I've of heard of those-'

'Yes, the page that Hyperion gave you, the one he'd written The Fallen on, it was taken from a book on the Relics. You see, it turns out that page wasn't aimed at you at all, it was a message meant for me.'

'What? But he told me I could be a Fallen, he wrote it on there-'

'So you would bring it to me. I thought it strange when you gave it to me, but I dismissed it, thinking he was just messing with your head.'

'But?'

'He wasn't, well, not just your head anyway.' Death crossed her pale legs, revealing a little bit too much thigh as Her red stiletto scraped the side of the coffee table. 'Yesterday we collected the soul of Lysithea, a Watcher whose particular field of expertise happened to be in the Apocalyptic Relics.'

I thought back to what Obadiah had said about the Demons' liking for the angelic Divine Spark. 'Was it a demon?'

'No, it wasn't a demon, although Lysithea had been slaughtered with Devil's Nightfall-'

'A demonic weapon?'

'Yes, although it was no demon who wielded it. The sword had Hyperion's musical stain all over it.'

'Isn't slaughtering angels against God's Will?'

'Yes, if it is found that it was, indeed, he who murdered and tortured Lysithea, Hyperion will be thrown out of Heaven.'

I thought I could hear the trace of something unsaid in Her words, a touch of sorrow maybe?

'It seems Hyperion doesn't care; he wants to bring about The End of Days so that he can challenge God's authority.'

'The End of Days?'

'Yes, you probably know it as the Divine Apocalypse. The time in which the One-hundred-thousand-year Truce will be broken, and the Four Horsemen will be let loose to ravage the earth, the time when men and angels must choose their side; Demonic or Divine, God or Lucifer.'

'And re-uniting the Relics can do this?'

'Yes.'

'But why does he need to Cleave his music? What has that got to do with the Relics?'

Death sighed loudly. 'Re-uniting the Relics would be a direct breach of the terms of the One-hundred-thousand-year Truce, it would cause a war, the likes of which, has never been seen before. When Hyperion cleaves his angelic music no one will be able to hear him coming. He will be neither Divine nor Demonic. He wants to destroy both God and Lucifer in the Apocalypse.'

'Hyperion wants to destroy God and Lucifer?' Could Hyperion really want to destroy the world as we knew it? 'Did he get any information from Lysithea?'

Death sat in silence for a moment, as though She were taking time over the words to use. She picked Her mug off the table before finally speaking. 'We do not know for sure, Lysithea was...tortured for a long while...her Arkhe had been partially removed...almost as though he was experimenting. We don't know how much She told him, but we can presume, from how she was left...'

'If you've collected her soul, couldn't you ask her, when she sits before God to be judged?'

Death shook her head. 'When I said we collected her soul...what I meant to say...well, it wasn't really a soul...but we have no word for the entity that he created, the thing that was left behind.'

This was the first, and only time, I had seen Death show even the slightest bit of uncertainty. For once She was not in control and, although She was desperately trying not to show it, whatever had happened, whatever She had seen, had disturbed Her. What had Hyperion left behind after he had tortured Lysithea? What on earth could possibly have scared Death, the Goddess of Mortality?

I didn't know, but if it had scared Her, then I knew I should be feeling terrified.

But I wasn't.

'Why do I need to go and see Obadiah again?'

'He holds the information you will need to stop Hyperion. We cannot let him re-unite the Relics. And do it quickly because we cannot let the Demons find out; we do not need a war with them, not at this time.

'Go to Obadiah, learn about the Relics, find out as much as you can about them. Then you stop Hyperion. Kill him if you must. He must not get those Relics, do you understand?'

I nodded.

'And Josh?'

'Yes?'

'Don't ever question my authority again.' she said, tightening Her hands around Her mug.

Evie

Revolution, the club where they were holding the engagement party, was like someone had eaten the 1980s and had vomited it all up over faux leather and glass. There were bright pink neon lights attached to almost everything, including the fake palm trees that were drooping either side of the bar like huge brackets in some unspoken sentence. I sat on a leather sofa upstairs, swirling my warm coke to determine whether the object floating on top of it was a slice of lemon, or something more sinister, whilst also trying to ignore the stares of a bald guy standing at the bar guzzling bottles of lager like they were going out of fashion. I'd never been too good at multi-tasking.

It was hot, too hot under the lights and the stares, so I grabbed my helmet and made my way over to the edge of the mezzanine, one sticky step at a time.

I looked over the clear Perspex balustrade as I took a sip of my coke. I could see Cassie on the dance floor, dancing provocatively in her stunning emerald green gown, slashed to the thigh, her red hair all elegant and curly as Ava Gardner. Celia danced next to her, her bottom falling out of the smallest hot-pants I have ever seen, her boobs almost doing the same out of her corset. She was a Highwaywoman, complete with a replica pistol and thigh high boots.

Dan, dressed as Jack Sparrow, pranced onto the dance floor and slipped his arms around Cassie's waist and started kissing her neck just as Laura Branigan started singing about self-control. The irony wasn't lost on me.

Watching their closeness, their obvious desire for one another, made me squirm. A thousand little worms wriggled in my stomach as she reached her hand up to his face. I closed my eyes, unable to watch them any longer. I suppose some of my disgust was down to the fact that Cassie was my mom - it was weird watching her do that kind of stuff - and it also hurt that Dan wasn't my dad, and she shouldn't be doing that with Dan, especially as Cassie was living off my dad's money.

But worse, worse was the fact that their intimacy exposed and opened up all of the deficiencies in me. I was alone.

And I was so fed up of being alone.

I could feel this gaping hole in my stomach, like all the stuffing had been knocked out of me. If I were a ragdoll, they'd just shove the stuffing back inside me and stitch me back up, or, more likely, they'd throw me away and leave me to rot.

Why was I still feeling like this? Surely I should be getting back to some sort of reality now? But then, most of me didn't know what was real or fake anymore. In my depression I had lost myself and I didn't know who I was or what was real.

I didn't know what I should be feeling.

Would the real Evelyn Anderson please stand up?

'Nice suit!'

I opened my eyes to find the bald bloke was standing beside me, his one hand resting on the balustrade, his other clutching a half empty bottle of Becks. 'Thanks,' I said, clutching my helmet tighter.

'I love Star Wars,' he said, sliding his body and his hand along the rail, moving himself closer to me, 'and I love Storm Troopers.'

'Oh,' I said, turning my gaze back to the dance floor just as Cassie and Dan began to snog. It was bordering on pornographic.

'Yeah,' said the guy next to me, now so close I could smell the tobacco and lager on his breath. It wasn't a good combination. 'I always wanted to be one, you know when I was a kid.'

'Oh,' I repeated. Maybe if I didn't say anything else he would get the hint and do one.

'Yeah,' he said, 'but I wouldn't look as good as you in it.'

As the words registered in my mind I turned to look at him, his face had gone weird, like he was going to eat me or something. I took a step back, clutching my helmet even tighter.

'Yeah, you look so good in those white heels. I love them, not authentic Storm Trooper, but still,' he said, licking his lips as he took another step towards me, his eyes fixed on my boots. It was official, he was freaking me out.

I don't think this was the outcome Celia had wanted when she'd turned up earlier that day with all the costumes; Cassie's emerald Ava Gardner gown, her sexy Highwaywoman ensemble (you couldn't really call it a costume as they wasn't much to it), Dan's Jack Sparrow and Carl's Indiana Jones complete with whip. She'd left mine until last, bringing it out of her Fiat in a black bin liner.

'Sorry,' she'd said, but I knew she wasn't at all, her eyes sparkled with mischief and her pencilled on eyebrows were so high that I couldn't see them and I wandered if she'd forgotten to draw them on, 'it was the last costume left in the shop.'

'Thanks,' I said, taking the bin liner and carefully opening it - not knowing what hideous creation she had got for me - desperately hoping it wasn't something like the Marshmallow man or an animal costume, or, even worse, something short and sexy. When I took it out I was actually relieved; I didn't particularly love it, nor did I hate it, but at least I could sneak off into a corner and not be pestered.

Or so I'd thought.

'Do you,' he said, trying to take the glass out of my hand, 'fancy getting out of here?'

I looked at him straight in the eye. 'Yes,' I said, turning and walking away from him, 'ON MY OWN!'

I didn't look back at him. Instead I struggled down the stairs, juggling my helmet and coke. My boots, as sexy as he thought they were, were a nightmare to walk in. And suffering in the name of fashion was not my thing, whatever Kylie, Kim Kardashian or any other celebrity said.

As soon as I got downstairs, I found the table that had been reserved for the VIP Engagement party guests and sat down, although VIP hadn't been intended for me as there were only four chairs at the table, but as the four of them were dancing, I didn't think they'd care. Cassie had obviously got other things on her mind, her tongue seemed to have been glued down Dan's throat for an eternity. I pulled off my boots and sighed in gratitude.

I looked at everyone drinking around me and realised I was in my own personal Hell. Dante's Inferno had got nothing on it. It was like all of my nightmares had grown legs and were now dancing around in front of me.

A movement in front of me caught my eye; Cassie and Celia had come back to the table.

'Hi Hun,' said Cassie, before she downed a half a glass of fake champagne, 'You okay?'

I nodded. I wanted to say, you've managed to prise your tongue out of his mouth then, but instead, I said, 'Are you enjoying yourself?'

'Of course she is,' cut in Celia, 'But you could make more of an effort.'

I smiled politely, 'Just having a rest, been dancing with a guy upstairs, now my feet are killing me.'

Celia stared at me. I wasn't fooling anyone.

'Okay Hun,' said Cassie. I really don't think she'd even registered what I'd said, 'I'm just going outside for some fresh air.'

'Okay,' I said, and off she sashayed.

And then I caught a glimpse of the bald guy, staring at me from across the dance floor. Geez, could this night get any worse? I grabbed a full bottle of the cheap champagne off the table and took a long swig. I could feel it trickling down the sides of my face.

I came up for air, wiping my mouth on my sleeve. What was I doing? Getting bladdered, that was Cassie's thing, and no way did I want to be like her. What was it Dexter had called her? A drunkard, a pisshead and a town bike, that was it. I thumped the bottle down on the cluttered table, the contents fizzed over the neck.

I was not like her, whatever Dexter or Amber, or anyone else thought. I was not a piss-head.

And then Cassie appeared in front of me, her hair blazing around her, her face wild, mascara tracing the tears down her face. She grabbed the bottle of cheap champagne and pretty much downed it in one.

She dropped into the seat beside me, her sobs lost to the music; Michael Hutchence was singing Never Tear Us Apart. This was their song; my father's and Cassie's. It was their first dance, their first kiss. Was that why she was upset?

'Hey, slow down,' I said, leaning over to her and putting my hand on her arm to stop her grabbing another bottle. 'Are you okay?'

'Do I look okay?' she snapped, wiping mascara over her face with her arm. I hadn't seen her like this for a while.

'I was only asking,' I said, grabbing my boots from the floor.

'Don't go,' she said, grasping my arm a little too hard, 'I'm sorry.'

I sat back down as she snatched another bottle.

'What's happened?'

She pulled the bottle from her lips and champagne dribbled down her front, blossoming across her gown like a blood stain. 'Dan. That's what's happened,' she spat, before downing more alcohol.

Of course she wouldn't be upset by the song, why would I even be as stupid as to think that? Cassie didn't think beyond Cassie. End of.

The bald guy came over. 'Hey beautiful!' he said.

I really didn't need it now. I was just about to tell him to do one when he grabbed Cassie's hand. 'No,' I said, pulling Cassie back as she stood up to dance with the creep.

'Jealous?' he sneered.

'No.'

'Leave me alone!' Cassie screeched, pulling her arm away from me, 'I can do what I want!' The creep led her away. It was painful to watch as he mauled her on the dance floor, his hands were all over her. It made me feel physically sick as he practically undressed her in front of me.

How the hell was I going to stop him? Where was Celia when I needed her?

Cassie's head fell onto the creeps shoulder and I could see him speaking into her ear. She nodded, and he led her off the dance floor and to the bar.

Leaving my boots and helmet behind, I followed them, keeping watch from behind a palm tree. I didn't know how I was going to get her away from the creep, but I knew I had to, because I didn't trust him one little bit. I trusted Cassie even less.

Two shots of Vodka were put down in front of them; they were both downed in a matter of seconds. Another two. No, this was hurtling way out of control.

I frantically looked around for Celia, Carl, a bouncer. Anyone. Anyone who could help.

No one.

Great.

Another two shots.

And then Dan appeared; Jack Sparrow running to the rescue. He pulled the creep off Cassie by his shirt. The creep turned around, his face twisted with rage. And there was Cassie in the middle, struggling to stand. The creep threw a punch at Dan but missed as Dan side stepped him. Dan turned to Cassie and began screaming at her.

Then the creep grabbed a pint glass and smashed it on the edge of the bar before swinging it at Dan.

'Dan!' I screamed, racing towards them. Dan moved just in time and the glass only grazed the side of his cheek. And then Carl and a few of the bouncers arrived. They were pulling the creep backwards, the glass lying at their feet broken and splintered but still sharp.

'Don't just stand there!' shrieked Celia, who'd appeared at my side looking like a screaming Erinye, an infernal avenger from Greek Mythology, 'Get over there, take her home!' She slammed Cassie's diamanté clutch bag into my chest.

Cassie was leaning over the bar, her eyes glazed. I grabbed her around the waist and urged her to move but it was like she was in another dimension or something, and her body didn't want to co-operate. I pulled her away from the bar, her head crashed onto mine, her full body weight pushing down on me.

I struggled across the club and headed out the front door. Outside was freezing, and drizzle was tumbling down from the sky, the annoying kind that soaked you to the bone in a matter of seconds. I'd forgotten my boots. I'd forgotten my helmet. But I wasn't going back.

A black hackney cab sailed past. I stuck my arm out and frantically waved him down, Cassie still holding on to me for dear life, unable to function on her own.

The cab pulled in further down the road and I tried to hurry Cassie along before someone nicked it. We caught up with it, the driver had the window down. 'Sorry love, can't take her. Not in that state,' he said, just as she vomited all over the path.

Great. 'Thanks.' I said, trying to fight the tears that were building at the back of my throat. Babysitting my own mother, it had to be the worst joke ever. No, I corrected myself, that would be my life.

By the time I'd dragged her home, nearly two hours, four cut feet and a pair of diamanté-covered shoes later, my tears had turned to anger. I managed to keep her upright as I opened the front door. I pushed her in through it, not caring if she landed on her face or not.

She kept saying to me 'I'm sorry, I'm sorry,' over and over again, but it was making the rage inside me burn brighter because I knew she didn't mean it, it was a stock response to a familiar situation. Not that I'd had to deal with her like this before, but hey, I suppose I was a grown-up now.

In the end I snapped. 'Shut up!' I shouted at her, but she was too far gone to even notice.

I shoved her on to the sofa, realising too late that she'd wet herself. This was supposed to happen when she was older, and I was old. Not now. I wasn't supposed to be cleaning her down now.

I couldn't leave her like that, I just couldn't, besides, it'd only make more mess which I'd have to deal with in the morning. I raced upstairs, grabbed a couple of towels from the bathroom and her dressing gown, then headed downstairs. I poured hot water into a bowl, clutched the soap and set to work.

Thirty minutes later she was lying on the sofa, clean (ish), and fast asleep under her duvet. But the anger inside me was alive, burning with the fire Cassie had fed it. I sat on the armchair just staring at her. She looked like a baby, tucked up in the foetal position, complete with the vomit dried in her hair.

I hated her. I despised her with a passion that I hadn't felt in such a long time.

But then, sitting there in the silence, with only my anger and thoughts for company, I realised that I was slowly becoming normal again - whatever normal was - but that scared me; too long in the wilderness and you lose the ability to be normal. I had to learn again, had to become human again.

Cassie started to mumble in her sleep, something about Dan and only wanting a cigarette, and the hate flooded my system again.

She wasn't my mother. My mother was long dead. She'd died along with my father, ten years ago. I couldn't change that, and right then, there was only room for hate.

I was her child, her blood, I'd been suckled on her breast and yet it made no difference. For once, just once, it would've been nice for her to notice me, to care about me.

I stood up and looked down on her. I'd had it with her. If Cassie was ill in the night it was her own dumb fault. I went to bed.

It was no surprise that Celia was pounding the front door early the next morning. I'd only got to bed at four, silly witch. The clock was now flashing seven-sixteen. I jumped out of bed, nearly tripping over the stupid Storm Trooper costume. I'd only got the the top of the stairs when she let herself in.

She looked up at me, 'Didn't you hear me?'

'Yeah,' I said, the anger still raging inside me.

'And?'

'And?'

'Where is she?'

'I dunno.'

'What?'

'Was the music too loud for you, has it damaged your hearing or something?'

Celia sneered at me before she turned and waltzed into the living room. I left her to it and went back into my room. I needed sleep. I slammed the door, grabbed the chair from my desk and shoved it up the handle. They weren't going to disturb me.

I fell straight back to sleep, that was one definite improvement since taking the tablets. The shadows now only haunted my dreams which had become vivid, bizarre and surreal.

The raven flew through my dreams, heralding the pitiful cries of a child which always cut deep into my soul. From where I lay I could see the full moon through the window, and then it was gone, obscured beneath a blanket of cloud. I climbed out of bed, the floorboards creaking under my bare feet, filled with the desire to look outside, to search for the source of the child's anguish. But, when I got to the window and looked out, I was staring into a void, a huge whirling mass of cloud and debris that devoured the babies cries. I stood at its edge, fear running through me. It was calling to me, urging me to step into its vortex.

I jolted awake, the echoes of the dream still swirling around me. I lay still for a moment, my body sweaty and trembling, my breathing ragged.

I rolled over. The clock flashed one in the afternoon; no wonder my stomach was angry at me for not feeding it, but did I dare go downstairs? Did I want to face what was down there?

My stomach told me I had to go, so I pulled my dressing gown on and made my way downstairs. I relaxed when I entered the living room and saw that Cassie and the duvet had gone, but my joy soon turned to dismay as I went into the kitchen to find her bent over a glass of water with a couple of aspirin in her hand. She looked up, her eyes were red and puffy.

'Oh, hi Hun,' she said.

I just smiled weakly at her and made my way over to the coffee machine.

'It looks like I've got some making up to do,' she said, to my back.

I put a pod in the machine, pressed the button and waited. I noticed I had a black bruise around my wrist, a perfect set of finger marks, probably off Cassie when she'd grabbed me in the club.

'I got it all wrong,' she said, cutting into my thoughts, her voice ragged and cracked like she'd been screaming for hours on end. 'It wasn't Dan...I thought I saw him outside, snogging a leggy blonde, but it wasn't...'

'Oh,' was all I could manage.

'Yeah, it turns out Carl's mate, Simon, had also gone as Jack Sparrow. It was him that was...you know.'

I could hear her fighting back the tears, but I concentrated on the smell of my coffee. I was not going to turn around. 'No, I don't know. What?' I asked, my knuckles turning white as I held onto the worktop.

If she heard the venom in my voice she chose to ignore it. 'It was him that was snogging the blonde. Celia told me, earlier, when she came around. What if Dan won't speak to me? What if I've lost him?'

'I'm sure you'll work it out,' I said, through clenched teeth. I couldn't look at her. I just couldn't. I piled sugar in my coffee, stuffed the biscuit tin under my arm, and then said, 'I need a shower,' and stormed out of the room.

There were no apologies for me, no thank you, no nothing. Don't worry about me bringing you home safely, cleaning up the vomit and the piss, I wanted to shout, but instead I said nothing.

'He's coming around later, to talk,' she shouted after me.

There were two scenarios that could happen and neither filled me with joy; The first - that she'd make up with Dan (which was highly likely as he was completely smitten, with her and her money) - filled me with dread because they'd be at it like rabbits for the foreseeable future and I'd feel uncomfortable in my own home making me want to throttle them both, or, secondly, they'd split up. This was even more horrendous as Cassie couldn't cope on her own, and more of last night would be the way she'd go. She'd drink and drink and disappear for weeks on end and I wouldn't know where she was until she turned up with some random and they'd be at it and I would feel uncomfortable in my own home.

Both scenarios were lose, lose for me.

I got to my room, plonked my coffee down on my bedside table and fell back onto my bed. I yanked the lid off the biscuit tin. Custard creams. I hate custard creams. I grabbed one and dunked it in my coffee, knowing my life

was just going from bad to worse.

Evie

12th August 2002, 2.38 pm.

The exact moment my happiness came to a crashing halt, when the threads of my life began to unravel. I mean the pure happiness you feel when you're young and evil still hasn't entered your world and everything is good and wonderful and simple. The place where Princesses are made and the monsters are slain and someone always comes rushing in to save you. The place where there is no grey, just black and white, good and evil. But evil never wins.

My father had been ill for ages, growing weaker and weaker as the cancer devoured him from the inside out, robbing him of his strength, of his dignity. But even as I sat at his bedside, his breathing becoming more laboured, the bruised skin hanging from his bones, I still thought someone, somewhere, would save him, that a doctor would come riding in on a white horse and tell us they'd found a magic cure.

Even after he'd gone, when his golden soul finally floated away from his body, I still didn't believe he was gone.

But he was.

Reality came crashing down on me a long time later, delayed maybe by my Gran's insistence that I shouldn't cry, that my dad was watching over me from his spot just behind the North star and he wouldn't like to see me cry; he wouldn't have wanted that. Not at all.

So I didn't.

I would never hurt my dad.

But how did Gran really know he wouldn't have wanted that?

She couldn't ask him, could she?

Only now do I see the elegant deception, the beautiful lie.

I would've done anything for my dad. I would've fallen on a sword for him. That was a fundamental truth, as day follows night or the sun follows the moon, and she knew it.

And still she used it as her weapon.

I don't hate her for it; she had a lot of mess to clean up after dad died, and at least Gran was there for me, not like Cassie. When Cassie was out enjoying herself, having her Second Coming, or whatever it was she called it.

'Hun,' she'd say, 'life is for living. As a wise man once said "eat, drink, and be merry for tomorrow we may die". Look at your dad, he was a good man and they still took him didn't they? You never know when your time is up, so enjoy every day like it's your last.'

And then she was gone, off out with the first of many of her male friends.

That was ten years ago, and nothing has really changed, except, now I don't have Gran and I don't believe in happy-ever-afters.

Josh

Threatening Evie's life? What a masterful stroke Death had played!

The bitch had me in the palm of Her hands.

I was trapped, set on a collision course with Hyperion, but what was in it for me? Nothing. Not even the chance of becoming a Fallen Angel. That's if I could believe what Death had actually told me, because, let's face it, I could trust no one.

Except Obadiah.

Going to see him would give me a perfect opportunity to find out about the Fallen. One way or the other I would find out the truth. Obadiah was the one certainty, the one angel I trusted. For I had seen it, in his memories, in his life story.

It seemed like an eternity had passed since I was last at Obadiah's, but it had only been a few weeks, and yet, so much had changed; the air was colder, the snow deeper, Obadiah's celestial music was weaker and my heart, my heart was now encased in stone.

I knocked Obadiah's door three times and waited.

I heard him shuffling behind the door and the sound of locks clicking. The door opened, revealing his bent silhouette in the doorway. He didn't say a word but signalled for me to enter with a flick of his crooked finger.

The old angel looked weak, much more fragile than when I had last seen him. 'Are you okay?' I asked, reaching out to touch his shoulder. The pain hit me before I'd even touched him, like a violent static shock, and thousands of images once again burned in my head.

I stood silent for a few minutes, waiting for the pain to subside and let Obadiah's memories settle into me.

'I'm good, what about you?' he asked. The smile on his face was tender, his milky white eyes warm and welcoming.

'I'm,' What was I exactly? I didn't know anymore, but settled on 'fine. Thanks.'

'I didn't expect to see you so soon, I haven't sorted out my affairs...'

I noticed the piles of books stacked all over the place. 'No, no,' I said, feeling a pang of guilt. I hadn't even considered how Obadiah might've mistook me visiting again. 'I haven't...I mean...I've just...Death's sent me, I need some information.'

'Oh,' said Obadiah, the sadness in his voice cutting me to the bone.

I'd done it again, hadn't I?

'Sorry, I-'

'No, no,' said Obadiah, raising his hand. 'You are welcome anytime. It's my fault. Please come in, sit down.' He gestured to the only wooden chair that was not struggling under the weight of dusty books.

'Thank you,' I said, tumbling into the chair.

'Coffee?'

'Yes,' I nodded, 'please.'

'Did you find what you needed at the Vatican?' he asked, shuffling over to the small kitchenette in the corner of the room.

'Oh, I found Hyperion,' I said, unable to keep the venom from my voice.

'Am I to take it he found the Necrodemonicon?' he said, placing a steaming carafe of coffee on the table with two mugs.

'I don't know,' I said, moving the pile of books on the chair next to mine so that Obadiah could sit down, 'but he destroyed the Castel, taking all of the Forbidden Library with it.'

Obadiah slid into the chair next to me. 'He destroyed it?'

'It was carnage. All of it, gone.'

Obadiah leaned forward, picked up the carafe and poured coffee into the chipped mugs.

'It's a very sad day when knowledge is lost.' He pushed a mug over to me.

'Thanks,' I said, wrapping my hands around the mug; it felt good to have my cold hands around something so hot.

'I remember them Nazis burning thousands of books,' he said, shaking his head. 'Once they're gone, they are lost forever. All that knowledge-'

'They'll be found,' I said, 'It'll take time, but all the books are still there, under the rubble.'

'Maybe,' he said. 'When I saw them books being destroyed by the Nazis, it ripped me in two. I vowed to myself, and to God, that I would save them, that I would rescue a copy of every single book that they tried to wipe out of existence.'

'Every book?'

Obadiah nodded. 'Yes, of all the thousands and thousands of books destroyed, Obadiah has found a copy of every single book, 'cept one, a book by Theodore Weiss. For that I am still looking. I have also been collecting other lost books, like them supposedly destroyed in the burning of the library of Alexandria. Over there,' he said, pointing to the shelves by the front door, 'are books by Anaxagoras, Eudemus and Prodicus.' He gestured to the far wall, 'over there are copies of The Book of the Dead, the lost plays of Aeschylus, and the Classic of Music by Confucius.' He slumped back in his chair and sighed.

All these book around him and he could not read one.

I wanted to ask him about The Fallen, I wanted to know if there were any answers in these books of his, if there was any hope at all, but all I could manage was, 'Death thinks Hyperion wants to re-unite the Apocalyptic Relics, that he wants to destroy God.'

'And you don't?' said Obadiah, his head tilted, as though he were listening carefully for my answer.

'It doesn't matter what I think. I've been sent here to find out what I can about the Relics. I don't come into it.'

'Sounds like someone has got himself mixed up in things he don't want to be?' Obadiah fell silent, his forehead wrinkled as his mind drifted off to another place.

'I saved the life of someone I shouldn't have.'

Those words brought him back to me. 'An Angel of Death saving a life? I hope the girl in question was worth it 'cause - and I know this only too well,' he said, with a wink, 'you're going to be repaying that debt for a long time.'

'A girl? Who said anything about a girl?'

Obadiah smiled, 'You know that whatever Death says, nothing will be good enough for Her. She won't let you go, no matter what. She'll follow you around like a smelly black dog.' He took a sip of coffee, before continuing, 'Yep, take it from Obadiah, She's like a dog with a bone.'

'You talking from experience then?'

A cloud descended over Obadiah, a heaviness had invaded his heart. 'Do you know what the Apocalyptic Relics are?' he asked, abruptly changing the subject.

'Nothing. Only that, when re-united, they can bring about the End of Days-'

'No, they don't bring about the End of Days in themselves. Don't they teach you angels nothing no more?'

'But Death said-'

'Yeah, well, as we know She says a lot and most of its shit.' Obadiah sighed, 'Let's start from the beginning. Grab that book on the end of the table. Over there,' he said, pointing to a stack of fragile books, their spines wrinkled and decaying, 'the one with the black cover. I think it's called Reliquiarum Sacrosanctum, Volume One.'

I rummaged through the pile until I found the volume he was after. 'Okay, got it.'

'Turn to page...' he rubbed the bridge of his nose with his fingers, 'thirty-three.'

I turned the groaning pages until I reached the section I needed. The gold decorative script at the top of the page read, The Apocalyptic Relics.

'You there yet?'

'Yep.'

'Okay, now read. Aloud.'

I cleared my throat, and began to read: 'The Apocalyptic Relics, or Sacred Triad, are three holy artefacts that God ordered the angels to scatter amongst men so that they might be hidden and kept safe until such a time they were needed. When the time is right, they will be gathered together again, breaking the terms of the One-hundred-thousand-year Truce, in order to raise the Four

Horsemen that will herald in the Apocalypse, a time when men will be brought to their knees in the Great War between good and evil, and they will have to decide on whose side they will fight; Demonic or Divine.

'It is said that the relics consist of The Spear of Longinus, the holy lance used to pierce the side of Jesus as he hung on the cross, The Holy Grail, the vessel in which Jesus served the wine at the Last Supper and The Key of Solomon, a most holy text that contains the spell that will allow the blood of Christ to flow from the spear into the Grail to conjure the Horsemen.'

'So now you see, it's not them Relics that bring about the End of Days, it's them Horsemen. Them Relics are just part of the ritual to conjure them.'

'But it doesn't help me, I still don't know where they are, or where Hyperion is.'

'No, but it's a place to start. Here, in this library,' said Obadiah, raising his hands in the air, 'you will find lots of information on them relics. Did you know that them Nazis were great relic hunters?' Obadiah leaned back in his chair, 'In fact, it is rumoured that they managed to find the Spear of Longinus.'

'The Nazis found the spear?'

Obadiah shrugged. 'Don't know for sure. But what I do know is that them relics don't have big signs on them telling everyone where they are. So Hyperion's after them; he has no more idea of their location than we do, not yet. But Obadiah has information here that can help. We start with what we have, what we know and work from there and why we are filling ourselves with information, Hyperion is out there, and he will show us his hand. He will search out the Watchers who have information on these things, do you think they will give up their secrets easily?'

'No.' I thought about Lysithea, about her murder and Death's reluctance to talk about it. 'Can we find the Watchers, wouldn't that be easier?'

'Unfortunately, even with all of these books, there is some information Obadiah can't lay his hands on. Do you know how many Watchers there are?'

I shook my head.

'There are thousands and thousands of them out there, and they all have their own little secrets to protect. For us to track the Relic Watchers would be like trying to find one particular speck of dust floating around the universe-'

'But Hyperion knows who some of them are.'

'He would, he is the Archangel of Wisdom, one of a only handful of angels privy to such information, and even He doesn't know them all. Even Death doesn't know.' suddenly Obadiah trailed off. He cocked his head to the side, his forehead heavily creased as he thought about what I had just said. 'How do you know Hyperion knows about the Watchers?'

'Death collected what was left of Lysithea, a Watcher who knew about the relics. The weapon that was used had Hyperion's scent all over it.'

Obadiah sighed. His wrinkled face seemed to age in front of me as he digested what I had said. 'I'm sorry to hear that. I've met her a coupla times, a long, long time ago, during the Council of Trent.' He turned, and seemed to look off into the distance. 'She was a good angel...an excellent Watcher.' After a few moments of silence he turned back to me.

'You mark my words, more blood will be spilt, and to find Hyperion we will just have to follow that trail of blood.'

Josh

I knew it wouldn't be easy to find Hyperion, not when he had the whole of the Heavens and Earth to play in, so I stayed at Obadiah's house, on a make-shift bed on the floor, spending every waking hour trawling through all of his papers and books, reading anything vaguely related to the Apocalyptic Relics, the Nazis, the End of Days. Obadiah, for his part, kept me stocked with coffee, and a never-ending supply of books. He was a fountain of knowledge, always producing a flurry of new leads, or new angles and ideas to try.

The quest to find Hyperion, to stop him getting the relics, became all-consuming, as if I were trying to replace my need for Evie with a new addiction. Or maybe it was because I didn't really want to look at myself, at what I was becoming.

Because inside I was dying.

At times the task looked impossible; how was I to know where the Relics were, where Hyperion would begin, or how many lives would be lost in his search? How was I, not even a true angel, a freak, supposed to stop him?

And, no matter how much I was possessed by my quest to find Hyperion, I never forgot about Evie. That wouldn't have been possible, however I tried to distract myself. My wings continually burned for her, burned for a love I never had, a love I would never receive.

My quest, my love for Evie, was all-consuming, a fever driving me on. I lost sight of myself, lost sight of Obadiah and what effect all of this, and my presence, was having on him.

A madness grew inside me, pulling me down into a dark, dark place. A place that, if I fell too far or too hard, I would never be able to escape from.

The madness grew strong, feeding on my neuroses, driving me to keep asking Obadiah about the mysteries of the Fallen. At first he avoided the subject, tried to get me to concentrate on the Relics, on the Nazis, on coffee, on anything other than the question I really needed answering. The one question that mattered above everything else.

And then one day I grabbed his hand. It trembled beneath mine, small, fragile, and yet with a strength that pounded through his veins like wild horses. 'I need to know about the Fallen,' I asked, looking up into his weary face.

'But-'

'Obadiah, I...I need to know. Not knowing is like a poison and it's driving me mad.'

The air became heavy and a sadness swept into the room, like an incoming tide, washing away the light, the hope.

'Come on Obadiah, I know you know something. Hyperion said it didn't have to be this way, that Death could've made me a Fallen-'

'Ignore anything he told you. He's too far gone, gripped in his own madness. His thinking is disjointed and confused. Just look at how his music is corrupted, at them evil things he's trying to do-'

'I need to know,' I said, cupping his shaking hand in mine. The pain was not so severe now, it had subsided into a burning sensation; painful but not all so consuming that it had me on my knees. 'I just need to know if it's possible.'

Obadiah shook his head. 'It's just the talk of a crazy angel.'

My hands fell away from his and I leaned back in my chair, defeated. I closed my eyes and imagined Evie stood in front of me, pictured the way her ebony hair fell over her shoulders, the way she walked, the smell of her skin, her emerald eyes. Even in my imagination she was beautiful, in reality she was breath-taking.

'She was seven when I first saw her. I'd gone to collect a soul, nothing unusual, just some guy who'd got cancer, like so many I have taken.' I paused, remembering the moment I first saw her. 'She was nestled next to him on the bed, her arm draped over his chest, her ebony hair cascading around her like a wild river. Her aura was so strong and pure like the light of a new born star. I was star struck.'

'It's unusual for a human to have such a pure aura.'

I nodded, but didn't look at him, too lost in my own thoughts. 'But that was nothing compared to her eyes. When she looked up at me, her emerald eyes took me off guard. They paralysed me, seduced me with their beauty. I knew she shouldn't be able to see me, but she did. In that one moment, that one look,' I clicked my fingers, 'my whole world changed forever. Inside me, it was like someone had kick-started my heart back to life. I knew it was love, though it shouldn't be possible...but still, it pulses around my body like the blood in my veins. She is my purpose, my reason, my life. Without her...' Finally I looked up at him, my eyes pleading with him to help me.

'Obadiah knows,' he said, smiling wistfully. 'When I first looked into my Nancy's eyes I knew I loved her...them eyes, oh them eyes were like amber kissed by the midday sun.' He smiled, and tenderly put his hand to his face, as though he was trying to recapture some long-lost moment. 'That was such a long, long time ago.'

'You miss her very much.'

He sighed again, it was long and mournful, almost like a cry of physical pain. 'Miss is such a small word for the hole she has left in my soul.' He opened his eyes and I could see tears gathering at their corners. He placed his hand on his heart. 'Sometimes...sometimes I think it could eat me alive.'

'I have loved Evie for all of my life, and my life before this, and maybe even the one before that, I just didn't know it until I had met her.'

'And she feels the same way?'

His words felt like a knife plunging into my heart and I thought my pain would come tumbling out of the freshly cut wound. 'She doesn't even know I exist.'

'But being a Fallen would not solve that. You cannot force someone to love you, and if she didn't, what then?'

'I-'

'She would die, you would live, alone, for centuries. Have you any idea what that feels like?'

'It's a price I am willing to pay. I would live a thousand lifetimes just for the chance...maybe she could love me...given time...'

Obadiah fell silent, regarding me with his unseeing, but all seeing, eyes. He flopped back in his chair, and sighed.

'Give me a moment,' he said, finally. He slid out from his seat and hobbled away.

It was only then that I noticed the subtle changes in Obadiah's music; it was growing weaker, almost like life was being sucked from it. I was draining him, in so many ways, and I knew I couldn't stay there much longer. One way or another something had to happen, something had to change.

'That is what you need,' said Obadiah, shuffling back into view, a small pile of papyrus held together by a bow of black ribbon. 'Them pages will tell you them answers that you seek.'

I took the pile of papyrus from Obadiah's hands and placed it on the table in front of me, staring at it, in awe of it, and yet, not daring to open it because of what its delicate pages might tell me. What if this was the end of the line?

I didn't look up as Obadiah said, 'I'll leave you to it,' and walked away.

The papyrus was burnt around the edges, like it had been in a fire, and it smelt of smoke and mould. I rubbed the soot away from the cover with my thumb, revealing the golden letters; The Mysteries of the Angels.

I pulled at the black bow and turned the first page over. The paper was as thick as card and yet fragile, the separate reeds beginning to unthread from each other on the edges. On the second page a list of contents were elaborately written on the paper in shimmering angelic script. I traced my eyes over it until I came to the section that I needed; On The Fallen. I turned the sheets, a heady mix of anxiety and excitement pulsing through me, like a child on Christmas Eve.

I began to read:

'The Fallen Angel is a most rare creature, an angel who has turned away from the love of God and, instead, has embraced the love of a mortal.

'The angel who wishes to fall must be pure, in both mind and body, so that they have a place in Heaven to fall from.

'The ritual of Falling is a simple one; first the angel must take an infusion of Asphodel before saying the words: Although changed, I shall arise the same. Finally, to complete the transformation, the angel must fall from a place of great height in a symbolic gesture of Falling from Heaven.

'The Fallen Angel will be stripped of their wings, and will be exiled from Heaven. After the ritual has taken place, a Fallen Angel cannot regain their wings, nor can they re-enter Heaven.

'This is the price a Fallen Angel must pay, for although God still loves them, their love for a mortal has supplanted their love for Him in their hearts. An angel, above all else, must have a pure heart.

'But, be warned, It is a treacherous and torturous path to tread; A Fallen Angel will know much suffering and pain as they outlive the mortal they have Fallen for.

'Once this path is taken, there is no turning back.'

I didn't even know I was crying until the tears began to pound on the papyrus like rain. So Death had told the truth; I couldn't become a Fallen. I pushed the papers away from me and let despair take me into her arms.

Hope was destroyed; only ash and dust was left.

I stood up and tipped over the table with a savage roar, sending the papyrus, books and coffee crashing to the floor as my rage unleashed like a hurricane.

I raced out of the house and into the cold New York night.

No more.

I couldn't do it.

I was finished.

So Death wanted a life? Well, She could have mine, the debt would then be repaid.

I would do as She asked; I would find Hyperion.

But I wouldn't stop him.

No.

If Death wouldn't destroy me, I would get Hyperion to do it. He had that power.

The time for reading and talking was over.

Wherever he was, whatever he was doing, I would find him and provoke him enough to destroy me.

I would get him to kill me.

Josh

Now all I had to do was find him.

I had studied many books dedicated to the Apocalyptic Relics. I knew that the Spear of Longinus, needed to induce the blood of Jesus, had been rumoured to have been found by the Nazis but where it rested now was a matter of dispute. Some thought it lay abandoned in Russia, others that it remained hidden in the bowels of Wewelsburg Castle in Germany, and then there were the thousands of other Spears that had been claimed to be that of Longinus, in places such as Rome, Vienna and Antakya. Where would I start? How did I know which lance was the true lance?

And then there was the Holy Grail; that too could have been hidden in one of many possible locations; from Rosslyn Chapel in Scotland, to Tintagel Castle or Stonehenge in England, or was it hidden in the bowels of the Louvre, the Sanctuary of Montserrat, or Malta?

Or the Key of Solomon? There were some who denied its existence, one scholar who claimed it was hidden in the Bodleian Library of the University of Oxford, another that it was in the personal collection of Samuel Gollancz.

And as for the trail of blood Hyperion would inevitably leave, thankfully, that particular river hadn't started running yet; there had been no other reports of unexpected deaths since the murder of Lysithea.

There was only one way to find him, even though it would be exhausting and like looking for a tear drop in the ocean; I would have to track down his music amongst the sea of other angelic harmonies. Finding him this way was going to be difficult, even more so than finding him at the Castel as then, at least, I had a rough location, an idea of where he had been. Now, Hyperion could be anywhere on earth or even in the Heavens, one discordant melody in a whole orchestra of angels.

I ran from Obadiah's house, knowing that there was no way he could follow, no way he could stop me. I cleared a few blocks before I stopped running, keeping a safe distance between me and Obadiah. The ground was covered in a thick blanket of snow, and in the sky, the thin sliver of the waning moon was barely glowing.

I concentrated on the blackest part of the night's sky I could find, let its darkness take my mind, let it anaesthetise my soul. Slowly, the Harlem skyline vanished - the trees, the townhouses, the apartment blocks - and with it the sounds of the city disappeared, until all I could hear was nothing but the harmonies of the angels near to me.

In amongst this angelic symphony I could hear Obadiah's sorrowful notes. I concentrated on this, allowing the music to transform in my mind, letting it take on shape and form until it twirled in front of me, a thin tendril of musical pain. I focused on it, allowing the other angelic tunes to develop behind it. Once all the parts of this celestial orchestra were fully formed, I pushed Obadiah's music away and allowed the other stems of angelic music to sparkle and dance in front of me, like a ghostly ballet. Thousands of interconnecting lines, almost like veins running through a body, ran across my vision; a visual picture of the celestial music of the thousands of angels in Heaven and upon earth.

In amongst the plethora of musical threads, I searched for the tainted, blackened tune of Hyperion, willing his song, and the visual interpretation of it, to reveal itself to me.

And there, barely beating in the sea of vibrant threads of life, was Hyperion's music, a raging inferno encased in a suffocating black tar-like substance. I concentrated on his blackened thread and started to let the other threads of beautiful angelic music fade away, until all that was left was the corrupted thread of Hyperion weaving through the landscape like a living compass point, a polluted umbilical cord of evil.

Filled with rage I took off, following the blackened thread through the landscape, like a wolf following the scent of its prey. It hissed and spit and scratched, a discordant melody of murder that fuelled my rage and the lust for my death further.

Soon I was flying over the Atlantic ocean, and although its deep water was calm, there was something sinister lurking in the air, something dark and unstable. And violent.

Hyperion's dark thread was pulling me across the sea, leading me towards the south-west corner of England, and straight into the heart of the violence.

As I neared the coastline, the sun's early morning rays were extinguished by a thickening cloud bank which rolled towards me from the east, and the stench of death hung heavy in the air. It wasn't my mistress' perfume, but a murderous aroma (a blend of iron, rusty copper and citrus; the scent of freshly spilt blood) that, I assumed, could only be coming from Hyperion himself. Beneath me thunderous waves were whipping up, raging against the jagged rocks, black walls of water standing like sentries protecting the rocky outcrop from intruders.

And right on top of the vertical cliffs stood Hyperion, burning brightly against the darkening sky like a miniature sun; a star plucked from the sky and speared to the earth. Beautiful and horrific, he looked like a General surveying newly conquered territory, his red claws clasped around a staff of iron. The ring of black that surrounded the interior of his aura was becoming stronger, I could see it burning ever deeper into his flesh.

I landed clumsily at the side of him, my anger raging inside me; I wanted to die, I wanted him to end it. And I would make him do it.

Hyperion didn't turn to look at me, but continued to study the demented waves.

'Beautiful, isn't it?' he said.

'What?'

'There used to be a castle, here on these rocks. If you look closely,' he said, pointing his staff at a crumbling wall of weather-worn stone, 'you can still see some of what's left, even after all of this time. Go on, take a look, I promise I won't bite. Yet,' he said, turning his head to look at me. 'No? Not playing? Okay, suit yourself. How did you find the book I gave you? Did it inspire you?' He flashed me a fiery smile.

'Is that your idea of a joke?'

'A joke? That's how you see my attempt to help you achieve your greatest desire? Well, that's gratitude for you.' He put a clawed hand to his hip, 'Haven't you even looked into it?'

'Yes,' I snapped back, 'I'm not a pure angel, I can't fall, I have no place to fall from-'

He pulled a face. 'Well, that's what She wants you to believe, it suits their purpose, don't you see? Keeps the little people in their place. If I were you, I'd try and look at the bigger picture, learn to think outside of the box,' he said, tapping the side of his forehead. 'Anyway, I haven't got time to solve all of your problems for you, not when I have my own to think about. Maybe you need to try and start thinking for yourself a bit more. I know as an Angel of

Death it's not your thing, but you know, everyone has to start somewhere.' He gave a shrug.

'What-'

'Shhhh!' he hissed, holding his fiery hand up to stop me speaking, 'I need to think.' He rubbed his forehead, like he was trying to smooth out the creases of his thoughts.

Above us the sky ripped open with a flash of lightning, and for a moment I could see we were standing on the edge of a small peninsula, adjoined to the mainland by jagged cliffs, a wooden footbridge being the only safe passage across. On the mainland, directly in front of me, great walls of crumbling stone zigzagged across the rugged landscape, and, nestled in behind them, amongst the grassy knolls and rocks, I could make out the buildings of the modern village.

'Here's a question,' he said, 'See that village over there?'

'Yes.'

'How long do you think it would take me to destroy it?' he asked, pointing his finger at the mainland, 'Go on, take a guess, it isn't a trick question!' He swept around to face me, his body leaving a trail of ghostly fire that hissed and spit in the bitter air.

Icy cold dread slithered down my back. 'You wouldn't.'

'Wouldn't I?' he said, flashing another smile. I could feel his breath brushing the skin on my face, leaving me cold, and yet hot, at the same time. My pulse raced, my breath quickened. Would he really destroy the village?

Yes, he would.

And I found the idea strangely enticing.

I was staring over a precipice of horror, knowing what was about to happen and not being able to stop it, being horrified by it but also captivated by it. And although I hated myself for it, the darkest part of me craved for the destruction. It wanted to be within the realm of death again.

'So,' he purred, 'how long do you think?'

I stared into his raging eyes, fighting the dark part of me, the destructive urge, that was pulling me in to those pools of fire.

'You're sick!' I said, pulling my eyes away from his. I turned away, I wouldn't be seduced by those eyes.

'No ideas?' he said. 'Oh come on, Josh!' he sulked, stamping his foot on the floor, 'You're being no fun at all!'

I wouldn't look at him. I couldn't look at him.

'Join me,' he said, raising his blackened hand to welcome me.

'NEVER!' I spat.

'Don't be so sure,' he said, 'I can sense that somewhere deep inside of you a war is raging.' He stepped towards me and stroked my face with his hand. It felt so good.

'I could give you everything you have ever dreamed of and more.' His voice was like honey. 'Evelyn-'

I felt myself drawn back to his golden eyes. 'No,' I said, but the word was weak, even to my ears.

'You could be with her, I could make that happen. For you.'

I felt myself falling into the pools of fire that were his eyes.

'I've told you,' I whispered, 'I can't be a Fallen-'

'I'm not talking about the Fallen.' He removed his hand from my skin, but I didn't want him to. I almost craved his touch. 'There are other ways. If you join me-'

'No,' I mumbled, but I was struggling; I was almost on my knees, begging for him to help me be with Evie.

'See that tree over there,' he said, pointing his staff towards a solitary tree, its bark covered in thick prickles, its branches twisted and deformed like his soul, 'that is the Thorn tree. The tree that grew from Joseph of Arimathea's staff when he planted it in the ground, the Joseph of Arimathea who brought the Holy Grail here from Jerusalem-'

'The Holy Grail is here?'

'Yes, and that tree is the marker. The Holy Grail is underneath us, Josh, waiting for us to claim it.'

'Why would I want the Grail?'

'Because if you place the Spear of Longinus over it, the blood of Christ will drip from the spear into the cup. That blood could make you immortal, would break the hold that Death has over you. And if Evelyn were to take a sip...'

He had my attention. What if this was a way I could be with Evie?

'You would be free to live your life with her. Just think of all the possibilities...'

It couldn't be that easy. Could it?

'You're lying.' But what if he wasn't?

'But you know I'm not. You know that if you place the Apocalyptic Relics together you can resurrect the Horsemen of the Apocalypse, don't you? Well, the same relics could bring you immortality. A life with Evelyn. And if Evelyn were to take a sip...Think about it...You and Evelyn, together, forever. You help me and I will set you free.'

That is all I had ever wanted.

'This is just the beginning Josh, come,' he said, holding out his hand to me again, beckoning me to take it, 'join with me.'

Lightning ripped the sky open above me.

What if he was right? What if the Grail could make me truly immortal, an immortal without a master. I could be in control of my own destiny. Maybe then I could make Evie love me. 'And what would you want in return?' I asked.

Hyperion stepped forward, his face tilted, his eyes sparkling with a deadly fire. 'That's the beauty of it Josh, you have to do nothing.'

'Nothing?'

'Exactly.' He lifted his staff in the air and the sea around us began to furiously rise up, great swirling masses of water standing to attention like soldiers of war.

'Don't do this,' I pleaded, barely audible over the thunder of the waves and the booming wind now thrashing around us. 'You don't have to destroy the town. If the Grail is beneath us, leave them, we'll go and claim it.'

He turned and smiled at me, his face wild with excitement, his eyes blazing.

The frenzied waves rose higher. The black clouds began to spew out their load. The air was volatile, excited at the prospect of Hyperion's rebellion. And in the midst of all this violence, Hyperion burned like a star.

A raging fire rising up in the darkening sky.

Lightning tore the sky in two, shocking me awake. I felt like I'd been asleep for a hundred years and was only now seeing the truth; whatever I did - whether I joined him or not - he was going to destroy the entire village. Could I really live with that?

'YOU CAN'T DO THIS!' I screamed after him, but my cries were lost to the orchestra of the storm.

Further he rose into the sky, the black frenzied waves rising with him. The darkness closed in on us until the only thing that was visible was Hyperion's brilliance, his arms outstretched; a burning crucifix alighting the night's sky. His hands were open as if he were pleading to God for help. But he wasn't pleading with God, he was defying Him.

Hyperion's voice became the storm. 'Come with me,' he thundered, 'taste the blood on your lips. Devour the spoils of war...We can be Gods Josh, you and I!'

If I joined him, this is what I would have to become.

'NO!'

I unsheathed Heaven's Will, my dagger, and, despite his fiery brilliance, I raced into the sky after him.

Too consumed by his own selfish desires, Hyperion didn't see me until I was on top of him, my left arm clamped around his neck, my right hand holding the dagger, ready to strike. I held on tight, fighting against the pain of his fiery flesh scorching my skin.

I stabbed him once in the shoulder.

Blood exploded from the wound.

The world shook as he screamed, a thousand suns exploding, obliterating all other sound. Hyperion's body ignited. My head was filled with the pounding of blood, the smell of burnt flesh, and a bloodcurdling scream.

It was my scream.

I couldn't hold on to him.

I let my body fall away from his, praying for Her to take me.

Praying that this would be it.

I wanted to die.

I fell through the air, until Hyperion caught me in his fiery net.

'YOU WILL DIE FOR THIS!' he screamed.

I smiled, my body relaxed as relief swept over me.

His face drifted out of focus. I was losing my mind.

Hyperion grabbed one of my wings in his claw-like hand and pulled. A sickening crack filled my head as Hyperion tore my wing clean off my body.

I closed my eyes and let myself fall, let my destroyed body plummet to the earth, praying that She would let me go. I wasn't strong enough. Didn't want to be strong enough.

I fell, my remaining wing flapping aimlessly in the wind as I hurtled towards the churning ocean. It reached up to me like a gigantic hand, promising me peace and solitude in its embrace. A watery grave of redemption.

But I didn't get that far.

I was falling, falling, falling.

Hurtling through the darkness, my body tormented with pain.

I don't know how long I fell; the seconds turned into minutes, minutes into hours, possibly those hours extended into days.

The only two constants were the pain and the darkness.

And through the darkness I heard Her screeching and cursing.

'Did you think it would be that easy?' She shrieked, 'Did you think you could escape me?'

I couldn't answer. I didn't know how to. Words had left me.

'You were supposed to kill him, Josh, how you have disappointed me. But then, you keep doing it, I should be used to it!'

The pain intensified and I was begging for Her to take me, but She just laughed.

'Not yet,' she sang to me, 'it's not over. Not yet.'

Evie

Dan had come around. They'd fought for a bit. I think a few things got smashed. I don't really know for sure because I kept out of the way, holed up in my bedroom and I didn't venture downstairs much, except to get drinks, crisps and chocolate. Not that they missed me; they were too busy shouting at each other or, making up, from what I could gather from the banging of a headboard and the groaning.

At times, I hated my life.

Being second best to my dad's memory would've been one thing (how do you even compete with a ghost?) but all her men too? Having to sit and listen to that?

I was trapped in a living nightmare, counting the hours until Cassie took off again.

But she didn't. And the banging seemed to go on. And on.

Like the demonic beast's war drum.

And I was alone.

But so close to someone who should have cared. But didn't.

The beast inside me was stirring. It slithered inside me, trying to get out, wanting to cause chaos. It whispered to me from the darkness, taunting me with its sadistic thoughts. And when I ignored it, it started to prod at my gut with a sharp stick. It had no intention of letting me go that easy.

I tried drawing, put my headphones on, the music turned up loud to drown it all out, but I could still hear the demon's pounding drum, its war cry. And it wanted to take me down.

But I couldn't let it.

I wasn't going to go back down into its dark lair, however hard it pulled on me with its suckered tentacles. A fire had been lit in the pit of my stomach and like most animals, the beast didn't like fire. I just had to make sure that fire didn't blow out.

I sat on the edge of the bed, hunched forwards, my hair scrunched tightly in my hands, praying for the banging to stop. I had to get out, and get away from them. I stood up, grabbed my hoodie and slipped downstairs unseen, quietly letting myself out of the front door. Outside darkness had tumbled down, a curtain falling over the forest of steel and brick. Rain drops splattered around me like tears on a page of a book, but I didn't know if I could turn the page. Maybe I was stuck in the horror story of my life, the demon snapping at my heels.

I started walking. I had to somehow break this cycle of crap my life had become. I wasn't completely ready for that challenge yet - I didn't even know where to start - but I knew that I had to make it happen.

I went back to the bridge, looking out over the black water, thinking about the time I had been at the exact same spot, just waiting to jump.

It all looked so different now, so alive under the heavy sky. A pair of swans glided like ghosts across the rain-pocked water and on the opposite bank a fox dashed for cover into the brush, splitting the night with its eerie high-pitched screech.

The clock began to strike twelve.

I could've jumped again. Finished it properly. Dexter couldn't save me a second time, could he?

But staring out from the bridge I realised that, although things were still the same, things had also changed. I had changed.

Death wasn't my only option anymore.

There was still fight - still life - left in me, whatever the beast said.

I looked up at the sky; there was no moon, no stars, just darkness.

Something caught my eye on the opposite bank. I couldn't tell what it was lying on the muddy river bank, but it was un-natural and out of place, a small mass of silvery light that shimmered weakly, almost as if a part of the moon had fallen to the ground and now lay dying.

I ran across the bridge towards the fallen moon, feeling its gravitational pull deep within my soul. It wasn't until I was sliding across the muddy bank that I realised that it wasn't a moon at all, but a man, curled up in the mud, covered in congealed blood.

A black tattoo ran across the man's back, a pair of wings that curled down as if they were folded back at rest. There was a long laceration on his right shoulder blade, correlating with the inside of the wing, it looked almost as if someone had tried to cut it out. There was a lot of sticky, blackening blood across his back and on the floor.

I turned him over slowly and felt his neck for a pulse; it was very weak but at least it was a pulse. His skin was ice cold and he was trembling; hypothermia was probably setting in. I had to get him to a hospital, and fast.

'Don't worry,' I said, 'I'm going to call an ambulance.' I brushed the matted hair away from his face.

His eyes flickered open, stunning me into silence; I knew him. Two beautiful eyes, like diamonds waiting to mined from the rock, looked back at me, weak but still full of life. His lips parted as though he wanted to speak but he didn't. Instead he let out a faint hiss as though even his breathing was too much for him, and then he let his head fall back, and closed his eyes.

'I need to go, ring an ambulance, I'll only be a minute-'

'No,' he whispered.

'You need to get to hospital-'

'No.'

'If you don't, you're going to die.'

'Leave me.'

I put my hands under his arms and carefully pulled him backwards, to the towpath beneath the bridge. I draped my hoodie over his trembling body. 'I'll be back...in a minute.'

'No,' he said, in barely a whisper, 'leave me to die.'

Something inside me broke at those words and a deep sadness washed into my soul.

I left him under the bridge and raced back to my house, knowing that I didn't have long, but I needed to do all I could to save him.

Once I was at my house, I let myself in through the back door. I slipped my shoes off, leaving them on the mat, and quietly hurried up the stairs to the bathroom. I grabbed a few towels from the cupboard, being really careful as I crossed the landing and passed Cassie's bedroom which had now fallen quiet. I went back downstairs to the utility room and rummaged through the clean washing, pulling out a pair of Dan's jeans and a thick grey jumper. I left a towel on the floor for when I came back.

Before long I was back under the bridge. The guy was still where I had left him, trembling in the mud. Somehow I managed to get Dan's jeans and jumper on him. He was caked in blood and dirt and looked in a really bad way. What if I lost him? What if I didn't do the right thing and he died?

'You need to help me,' I said, 'I can't carry you on my own.' I felt tears building at the back of my throat. I forced them back down. Now was not the time to cry like the pathetic little girl I was.

He nodded but didn't open his eyes. I managed to drag him off the floor, but slipped back in the mud, covering my jeans in blood and dirt. Eventually I got him up the bank and onto the path, trying to hold up his weight as much as I could.

The rain started to fall faster as we stumbled down the road. And all I could think of was that he couldn't die because I couldn't even remember his name.

When we got home, the lights were still off, so I pulled him through the side gate to the back door. I felt his cold body pressing down on me as I fiddled with the lock and I knew I had to save him.

Somehow I managed to quietly drag him up the stairs. When I got to my room I let him fall onto the bed. I collapsed next to him, completely exhausted, but I knew I had work to do, so I hauled myself back up. Before I left, I pulled the duvet over him, and then went to see what damage I'd caused downstairs.

It didn't appear to be that bad. I mopped the kitchen floor, shoved the dirty towels straight into the washing machine and went to clean myself up in the shower. For the first time in my life, I hoped that when Cassie came down in the morning she'd be too loved up to notice if I'd left any mess.

It was two-thirty in the morning before I managed to crawl back to my room, half expecting him to be gone, just a figment of my crazy imagination.

He was still there, curled into a ball, trembling under the duvet. I climbed onto the bed and curled up next to him, on top of the covers, like it was the most natural thing in the world, like we weren't strangers, like I'd known him forever. I should've gone to the spare room, should've slept there, but something inside me craved to be close to him, needed to pretend, if only for one night.

It was stupid and reckless - bringing him home, sharing a bed with him - but I didn't care.

I didn't even know his name, and yet I was lying next to him, sharing my body warmth, my sacred space. It felt good to be so close to someone.

I wish I could tell you that saving him was the most un-selfish thing I have ever done, but the truth was the complete opposite. Everything I did that night was for me. I was saving myself. I just didn't know it.

Evie

He had to go.

I was being needy.

I was being stupid.

I was being Cassie.

And, I couldn't be Cassie, jumping straight from one guy to the next, and that's what it felt like in the cold light of the morning. It scared me how easy I had fallen into the trap. Dexter didn't want me, so what did I do? Go and bring home the first stranger. Stupid, stupid, stupid!

As he showered, I lay on the bed, listening to the silence, punctuated only by the sound of running water. There was an empty space beside me, the dirt and blood smears the only evidence that the night had been real, that it hadn't been a dream.

But now it was over.

I got up and switched the television on, a distraction from thinking and to hide our voices from Cassie. I turned as he walked back into the room. My eyes caught his. My heart stopped. I couldn't breathe.

I finally managed to look away. He turned to close the door and my eyes were drawn back to him. Water was dripping from his hair, running like tears down his skin and over the intricate tattoo wings that swept down his back, the tips of which were lost below the towel he was clutching at his waist. I suddenly felt hot, my skin flushed. I tore my eyes away, too scared to look, even though I wanted to.

My body was on fire, my emotions loudly screaming at me, pulling me in different directions.

I saw him turn around out of the corner of my eye. 'I'm sorry,' he said.

'For what?' I said, looking up, my eyes captured by the sight of another intricate tattoo carved onto his chest which I had missed the night before, when it was caked with mud. It was another pair of wings, but this time with a skull at the centre of the design, with a silver dagger behind it. What was it with this guy and wings?

'For everything.'

'I'll get you some clothes.' I needed to get him out of the house. There was some kind of witchcraft in the air, it was pulling me in, enchanting me. I had to ignore the feelings bubbling up inside me, making my skin tingle, my breath quicken.

Those eyes were goddamn killing me. Why couldn't I be in close proximity to a guy and not want to kiss him? Kiss him? I instinctively looked at his lips. God, I was feeling really hot.

'Thanks.'

I grabbed my dressing gown and slipped it on. I moved towards the door, then stopped. 'You'll have to leave when it's safe,' I said, not daring to look back at him. 'They can't find you here.' I couldn't leap from one guy straight to another.

'Ok,' he said. I thought my heart was going to break. Stupid, needy Evie! What the hell was wrong with me?

Downstairs Cassie was sitting on the sofa, her hands curled around a mug of coffee, her hair pulled high in a messy pony-tail. Dan was next to her, messing with a stray bit of her hair at the back of her neck.

'Oh, hi Hun.'

'Hi. How are things with you guys?' I asked, trying not to look guilty. I shouldn't have bothered; Cassie was always more happy talking about herself.

'Well,' she said, reaching over to put her mug down on the coffee table before she grabbed Dan's hand. 'As you know, things, well, we kind of got off track there for a bit, but everything's good now.' She turned to look at Dan, her eyes brimming over with love, and for a moment I was overtaken by how much I despised her. 'We're going away for a bit, to Dan's parents in Cornwall, see if we can find any good wedding venues.'

'Oh.'

Eventually she prised her eyes away from him. 'I know we haven't been back long Hun, but we want to get married as soon as possible. We want to bring the wedding forward...to be married now.'

'Ok.'

'No more misunderstandings,' she said, her eyes fixed back on Dan.

'When are you off?' I asked, my emotions all battling it out for supremacy; relief, hatred, jealousy, sadness. I didn't know what I was supposed to feel; I just wasn't used to it. But my guilt at having a strange guy in my bedroom evaporated under the strain of everything else I was feeling.

'Next weekend. We're going for a week so you'll be on your own over half-term, unless you want to come with us?'

'Who me?' I said. I never usually got invited. Why ask this time?

'Well you are going to be bridesmaid.'

'No, I'll stay here. You don't want me cramping your style. We can do the girly stuff when you get back.'

'Ok Hun, if you're sure. See Dan, told you she'd be fine with it. She's a good girl.'

Those words stabbed me through the heart.

She's a good girl.

How would you know Cassie, how could you possibly know? I stood up, 'I'm going back up to my room, I've got a lot of work to do.'

'Ok Hun,' she said, not taking her eyes off Dan.

Evie

I grabbed angrily at Dan's clothes in the utility room - pulling out his favourite denim jeans and Ben Sherman jumper - before I stomped back upstairs. My anger was festering inside me. I was a good girl. A good girl! That woman made me want to scream. Or worse!

I yanked open the door to my room, my anger set to unleash on my mysterious stranger, but I stopped as my eyes caught sight of him, lying awkwardly across the bed, asleep. He wasn't supposed to fall asleep, he was supposed to be leaving.

But he looked so worn out, so broken and oh so beautiful, that my anger evaporated. A calmness had swept over my room, like when you're on holiday, sitting by the sea on a hot summer's day, with the breeze rolling in off the ocean, keeping you cool and calm and there isn't a single cloud in the azure sky. That's how I felt looking at him, his chest rising and falling like the ebb and flow of the tide and his sun-kissed skin like the sand at my feet.

I dropped Dan's clothes on the floor and went to the airing cupboard, pulling out a blanket to drape over him.

I went for a shower to cool off, and to distract myself, but it didn't work, knowing that he (temptation? because that's how it felt) was just the other side of the wall.

I went back to my room, sat at my desk, flicking a pencil to and fro in my hand. I fetched out my English essay, but I couldn't concentrate; the sound of his breathing, delicate though it was, invaded my thoughts and made me picture the ocean, made me want to walk in the gently lapping water. I put the essay to one side and started a sketch for our new art project (An Angelic Journey through time: the changing face of angels) but found myself stealing glimpses of him, until, in the end I gave up, with barely a pencil mark drawn on the paper.

I swung my chair around, put my feet on the bed, my head resting on my hands, and just watched the rise and fall of his chest, let my breathing synch with his, let his tranquillity wash over me.

I don't know how long I sat there for - time had simply ceased to exist - entranced by his face, by the shape of his nose, the curve of his chin. When he rolled over, the blanket fell away slightly, revealing the magnificent tattoo on his back, I couldn't stop tracing the delicate strokes of the design with my eyes. How I longed to trace my fingers over it, feel the softness of his skin under my fingers, let my hands sweep down his back to the tips of his wings, lost just below the top of the blanket.

He was like an angel. Never mind all the pictures of angels in my art books, his face was the most beautiful of all.

Or was he the moon, and I the sea, his gravitational pull too strong for me to ignore?

I was going crazy.

Without thinking, I carefully moved forward onto the bed. I reached out to touch the marks on his back. There was something about them, something about the way they seemed to almost ripple under his skin as though the wings were waiting to hatch. I just wanted to make sure they weren't real. And then my heart stopped, my hand mid-air, as he turned over.

His eyes were still closed, his black hair swept across his face and he looked more like a marble statue than a guy (I thought of the God Apollo, or Perseus that I'd studied for Classics. Or was it Michelangelo's David?).

My eyes wandered to the tattoo on his chest, another set of wings with a skull and dagger. I extended my fingers to touch; I couldn't help it. I let my them fall onto his soft skin - even though I knew I shouldn't - and began to trace it. The lines of the tattoo surprised me, they were ice cold to the touch unlike the rest of his burning skin, and they too seemed to ripple with an energy, almost like they were alive. My fingers lingered as I reached the skull, intricately cut into the skin above his heart. I could feel his heart pounding beneath my fingers.

And then he clasped my wrist with his burning hand and my whole body burst into life. My heart stopped, my eyes sought his, and they startled me with their brilliance.

'I...I'm sorry,' I said, moving my hand from his chest, his fingers still wrapped around my wrist. Our hands hovered mid-air, neither one of us wanting to pull away. I was electric; I could feel every single nerve, every single sensation in my body. His touch penetrated deep inside me, shocking me awake, pulling me out from the shadows, re-awakening abstract feelings and memories deep within me that I couldn't quite remember but I knew they were there, still buried waiting for me to discover them.

But I remembered his name; Josh. The name was made for me. It fitted my lips perfectly.

I was on fire.

We hovered in that moment, the air around us alive with anticipation. There was something building between us, something drawing us together in this small space, this obscure un-real situation.

And I knew - from that one moment that seemed to last for an eternity - that he felt the same way.

I wanted to kiss him.

I knew he wanted to kiss me.

But his closeness, my lack of control, scared me. I wasn't going to be weak. I couldn't give in. I was not Cassie. I wasn't ready for this.

I pulled away. 'You need food and painkillers,' I said, tearing my eyes away from his.

Cassie and Dan were back in bed, so I went downstairs and made a huge pile of toast, a pot of coffee and stuffed them onto a tray with two mugs, sugar, milk and a box of ibuprofen. I took a deep breath and entered my bedroom, trying desperately not to look at those eyes.

'Bugger,' I said, to myself as my eyes met his. I took a sharp intake of breath and my heart rolled in my chest. I was out of control, my body not listening to anything I was telling it to do.

He was sitting on the bed, propped up against the headboard. He'd pulled on Dan's jeans which seemed to be too short for him, the towel discarded on the floor at the side of the bed. Suddenly I felt really hot again.

I walked to the bed and dropped the tray down, trying to hide my face so he didn't see me blushing. Butterflies were flying around my stomach and I noticed my hands were trembling.

'I thought I'd make you some breakfast, even though it's more like afternoon now. Didn't know what you like so I did a pot of coffee and toast, because everyone likes coffee and toast. Don't they?' I looked up and caught him looking at me; my body tingled under his gaze.

'I'd love a coffee,' he said.

'Grab some toast and I'll pour you a cup.'

'Thanks,' he said leaning over to get a slice. Every time he moved there seemed to be a ripple effect in the air that sent waves of longing through me.

I left his coffee on the tray, picked up mine and a triangle of toast, and sat on the chair by my desk, placing my feet on the edge of the bed. I couldn't trust myself to sit by him. I needed to exercise some self-restraint.

Maybe I was more like Cassie than I thought?

'You can stay here tonight,' I said, 'but you'll have to leave tomorrow, once I've gone to school, when Dan and Cassie are out.' What was I saying? He was supposed to be leaving! It was like my head and my heart had split in two and were fighting each other for supremacy.

'I'll go-'

'In your state? Don't be stupid. Stay here,' I said, quickly adding, 'Just for a bit.'

Being in this room, being so close, it was starting to chip away at my resolve. There was something in the air, something I could almost reach out and touch, that was luring me in, like following the devil through pits of fire just for a moment's pleasure.

I think my heart had the edge.

I didn't know if I was strong enough to resist.

We both sat watching the television. Something terrible, a freak storm or something, had wiped out an entire village down south.

Josh made a strangled sound. I looked up at him, his face had turned ashen. 'Are you okay?' I asked.

'I'm fine,' he said. But the way he said it made my heart heavy, it was like how I imagined the angels mourned the dead.

I went over to him and sat on the edge of the bed. I leant over and placed my palm on his forehead. I was very aware that our bodies were almost touching. I felt his heart beating, the electricity leaping through what little space there was between us.

'You're really hot,' I said, blushing as I realised what I had said. I looked away, before adding, 'You need painkillers.'

What the hell was I doing?

Josh

I had once heard someone say that life was like playing a game of chess with Death, that it was down to us as to how well we played and how long it would last.

What a crock of shit.

We're in check mate from the moment we're born.

Only the ignorant and idiots believe anything different.

Death cradled me in Her arms for what had seemed like an eternity; an everlasting darkness that robbed me of everything but my pain, and then, when She was ready, She had relinquished me, let me fall to earth and into Evie's arms. She'd done it on purpose, leaving me on the river bank - broken and as close to death as was possible - for Evie to find; the only person, Death knew, that could make me want to live, and make me want to fight Hyperion.

When I finally awoke, I didn't even need to open my eyes to know Evie was there; the pain, like walking over the blades of a thousand swords, coursed through me, to the thrumming of her heart beat. Bitter yet sweet.

I wanted to run.

I should've run.

But my body was wrecked. The pain of being close to Evie, and the pain in my muscles, deep in my shoulder blade where Hyperion had torn off my wing, was burning as brightly as it had ever been, but I knew, somehow, I had to find the strength to fight it.

I grabbed a piece of toast and looked up at the television, something had drawn my attention, the mention of a storm, of a village decimated by an unusually high tidal surge that had sent huge waves crashing down upon it, wiping out everything in existence. I stopped, toast at my lips, as I recognised the place. I watched the screen, transfixed as my fellow Angels of Death reaped the dead, their celestial melodies playing, only to my ears, as a backdrop to the news report. The dead sang too, lamenting the loss of their own lives, their Souls shimmering in the sky, only a rainbow to the human eye.

I watched as Arielle, dressed in a gown of black silk, prepared the soul of an old man whose turquoise aura was beating brightly despite his old age. Kazuo - a handsome angel with ice blue eyes - washed the golden brown soul of a seventeen year-old girl, whose pitiful song was of regret and things left un-done, and things never to be done.

The female news reporter, in full make-up and a perfectly coiffured bob, stood in front of what was left of a hotel, the sun's rays penetrating through the cloud, like gigantic fingers of gold around her.

'Three-hundred and thirty-three people have known to have died in the freak storm, over one-hundred are still missing. Experts are still baffled as to how the storm appeared out of nowhere and caught the Met office off-guard.'

'Are you ok?' asked Evie, breaking my fixation with the news.

'I'm fine,' I lied. What else could I say? I caused all of that, all that death and destruction...oh, and by the way, I love you. I took the painkillers she offered me and gulped them down with mouthfuls of dark sweet coffee.

There was a long stretch of silence, filled only by the murmurs of the never-ending experts and reporters on the television. it wasn't an uncomfortable silence; it was loud, filling the air with things thought but not said, feelings that were screaming at us, trying to get us to acknowledge them.

'What happened to you?' she asked, finally cutting through the silence.

The question took me by surprise. 'What?'

'On the river bank, what happened? Do I need to be worried? Some scary gangster isn't going to come after me for helping you?' she asked, only half joking.

I shook my head. 'I got in trouble and paid the price, but no, you don't need to worry.'

'Is it over?'

I looked in to her emerald eyes; I just wanted to reach over and kiss her. 'I don't know,' I lied, knowing full well it wasn't. More lies and I hated myself for it.

'So, who are you? What do you do for a living? Are you my Guardian Angel? Because you seem to appear when I need you.'

My heart stopped beating for a moment. Did she need me? I didn't think I'd ever be able to leave if she did, and I needed to leave.

'You make me sound like a stalker!' I laughed, trying to shake the comment off, but I seemed to choke on the words. 'I'm no Guardian,' I said. 'Anyway, you saved me last night, remember?'

'Maybe,' she said. 'So?'

'So?'

'Go on then, spill the beans, what do you do Josh?' she asked, looking back at me.

The way she said my name was driving me crazy.

'I find things for people, old books and stuff-'

'Sounds mysterious, like Indiana Jones?' she asked, a mischievous sparkle in her eyes.

'Are you making fun of me?'

'No,' she said, placing her hand on heart, 'well, maybe, just a little.' A cheeky smile lit up her face.

I shook my head and smiled back. 'No, I'm not like Indiana Jones.'

'That's a shame, I quite fancy Indiana Jones.'

I looked at her, but she turned away, before our eyes found each other.

'I don't usually pick up complete strangers who have been beaten up and take them home,' she said, looking at the coffee mug she nursed in her hands.

'Oh, I thought it was like a hobby or something-'

'No...It's not like me at all.' She fell silent, still studying the contents of her mug.

'Thank you, for looking out for me.'

Finally she looked at me again. 'That's ok...I'd do it again...in a heartbeat.' Her eyes were almost pleading with me, searching for something. 'Anyway,' she said, finally tearing her eyes from mine, 'I need to do some homework, if that's ok?'

'You don't need to ask me, I'm only a guest. I could do with some sleep anyway.' I continued drinking my coffee as she swung around in her chair. She tied her ebony hair in a messy pony-tail then pulled out a large piece of paper and began to draw on it with charcoal.

I couldn't keep my eyes off her, the way she crossed her legs under the desk, the curve of her back as she leaned over to draw, the way her pony-tail swayed as she moved, the light from the window highlighting the pale skin of her neck. I held tightly onto my mug. How different things could've been if I wasn't a freak, if we could be together. If she had actually wanted me.

'Let's have a look,' I said, dropping the mug down on the bedside table.

'Not yet, it's a bit rough,' she said, without looking back at me.

I pulled my legs out of the bed and swung them around to sit up on the edge. I caught sight of the picture she was working on.

'Wow.'

'It's for a project in art. Angels through time. I'm going for the Gothic look.'

A lump caught in my throat as I looked at the picture; an angel (a self-portrait of Evie herself, perhaps?) slumped in the middle of the paper, tears running down her cheeks.

Angels? Really? What a sick twist of fate.

'You're very talented-'

'You're just saying that.'

'No. No, I'm not,' I said, studying the smudge of charcoal on her cheek. It was getting a little too hot for comfort in her bedroom, despite the pain, just being close to her was making my back burn and I just wanted to...

She turned back to her work, but I stayed on the edge of the bed. A few stray hairs on the back of her neck caught my attention. I wanted to move them, let my fingers brush over her skin as I did so, let my lips trace over the base of her neck.

'What's up, have I got something on me?' she asked, feeling the back of her neck with her hand.

'No. Nothing,' I said, guiltily.

'Then what're you looking at?' she said, turning to face me.

'Nothing, honestly.'

'You're putting me off,' she said, smiling.

'Sorry,' I said, holding my hands up, 'I'll just lie back down.'

'That might be a good idea,' she said, laughing as she turned around.

I lay back on the bed, my soul aching for her to lie down next to me.

No, it was all so wrong.

When she went to school tomorrow I would leave, never come back. It was better that way. Death would not win.

Evie

When I woke the next morning, I kept my eyes closed for a moment, not wanting to open them, not wanting to break the spell, but eventually I knew I had to, I couldn't stay there forever.

Life doesn't stay still for anyone or anything.

We'd somehow both fallen to sleep on top of the bed. Josh was still lying next to me, his eyes closed, his chest rising and falling gently. I watched him for a while, then bent down to kiss him tenderly on the forehead, letting my lips linger on his skin, inhaling his sweet scent that reminded me of honey. I committed it all to memory so that I knew that this had once been real.

This was my goodbye; when I got back from home he would be gone.

I left the house - Dan and Cassie were still in bed - and rang Sam; I couldn't be on my own today, I needed a distraction to keep me from thinking about the hole opening up in my gut, and the hours rolling out in front of me before I went back home and found that he'd gone.

I told him to leave, right? So why did I feel so crap about it?

Jesus, I was frickin crazy. And frickin needy.

How was anyone else supposed to keep up with me when I didn't know what I wanted myself? The only thing I did know for sure was that I didn't want to be Cassie.

I met Sam for breakfast at Sofia's. He was already there, sitting in a booth by the window, stuffing himself with American pancakes and an espresso. I just had a latte - I couldn't stomach anything else - my body and my mind were distracted, back at home. In bed with Josh.

But I had to forget him. I would not allow myself to be Cassie.

'Hey, earth to Ev!' said Sam, pushing my arm gently.

'Oh, sorry,' I said, feeling the flush of red crawl up my face, embarrassed at what I'd been thinking about right in front of him. It almost felt like my mother was in the room.

'Bad night?' he asked, 'They been at it again?'

I nodded, then looked away quickly before he saw through my lie. And now I felt ashamed that I was just getting my best friend back and I was still lying to him. No, not lying exactly, but I wasn't telling him about Josh was I?

It was my dirty little secret. And that's the way it would stay.

'Come on,' he said, 'we better get to school and hopefully your brain might catch us up on the way.'

I smacked him on the arm, 'Funny!'

'I try,' he said, as we left the cafe. Outside the dark sky threatened rain, so we hurried to school, arriving at the gates just as the storm started; sheeting rain accompanied by thunder and lightning. Sam and I held our bags over our heads and ran for class.

After Registration, we all headed off to English and preparation for a timed essay which I'd completely forgotten about. I sat down at my table, and grabbed my pens, pad of notes, and book out of my bag. I looked at the white-board, and the question scrawled across it in red pen:

"What is the role of the half-being in Carter's stories? What does their liminal experience tell us about our own human experience? Include at least two of the following types of character: werewolf, vampire, beast, feral child."

I knew I'd read something, somewhere about it. Something about the liminal character facing torment because they don't belong in reality or in the un-real world, or was it something to do with questioning gender roles?

How was I supposed to know?

I stared at my book hoping for inspiration, but my mind wouldn't co-operate, it kept drifting off to my bed, back to Josh. I kept picturing him lying there asleep; his naked chest above the covers, revealing his wings. My skin tingled as I imagined lying down next to him, placing my lips on his. I couldn't believe how alive I felt, every part of me seemed to respond when I thought about him. With all this going on, how could I concentrate on a stupid essay?

After so long feeling nothing, these feelings and emotions were flooding my system, and I was becoming addicted to them; I only wanted to think about Josh. I wanted to stay in that dream forever.

I had never felt like this about Dexter.

I looked over to him. He was hunched over his pad of paper, scribbling notes, Amber sitting beside him. She looked up at me, her eyes locking on to mine, and for once I didn't look away as she glared, her nostrils flaring like a bull that was about to go on a rampage. It wasn't pretty.

Mrs Jones coughed, so I turned back around and looked at my notes, but I wasn't actually reading them.

Was I really that fickle to transfer my feelings from Dexter to Josh? Was I really that tragic?

I looked back at Dexter - this time free from Amber's gaze - and watched his hand move quickly over his notepad, watched the way he stuck his tongue out over his bottom lip as he worked, and I felt nothing.

Absolutely nothing.

And yet, Josh, he made me feel alive, like I'd known him forever.

The bell went for break and I brushed everything off the table and into my bag. Amber rushed past, roughly bumping into me.

'Something smells around here,' she said, grabbing onto Dexter's hand before they left the room.

'Don't worry about her,' said Sam, coming to stand beside me, 'how did you find it?'

'Er, what?' I asked, my mind wandering out of the door with Dexter and Amber, and back into bed with Josh. 'Oh, the essay planning? Yeah, fine,' I lied. Again. I was getting far too good at that, and I needed to stop it. 'Come on, let's get something to eat.'

We both made our way to the cafeteria. I grabbed two toast, and a bottle of water, then sat down as far away as I could from Amber and Dexter. Sam sat next to me with a plate full of scrambled egg on toast.

'You've had breakfast already,' I said.

He shrugged. 'What can I say? I'm a growing boy.'

I rolled my eyes at him and took another bite of toast.

'You don't still have a thing for him do you?' he asked.

'Who?' I said, pulling my gaze away from Dexter.

'You know who. Dexter.'

'Dexter? No, who said I had a thing for him?' I asked, not looking at Sam but instead taking a mouthful of water.

'Come on Ev, you've been staring at him constantly this morning. And after what he did to you the other day? What's going on?'

'Nothing.'

'Amber's been telling anyone who'll listen that you're stalking him.'

I looked up at him and pulled a face. 'As if.'

'Well, you're doing a good job of proving her right, staring at him is a bit desperate-'

'Desperate?' I asked, my voice incredibly high. 'I am not desperate.' I slammed my water bottle onto the table a little too hard so that some of it splashed over my hand.

'Ok, ok!' said Sam, holding his hands up in surrender, 'But you do fancy him?'

Was that a statement of fact, or a question? 'No.'

'Are you sure?' he asked, his eyes narrowing as he looked at me.

Was I sure? I looked over at Dexter who was laughing at something Kieran had said. Amber was missing. Dexter looked up, catching me looking at him, but I didn't look away. I just stared at him. Eventually he looked away and started playing with his phone. Dexter had never looked at me in the same way Josh did. It didn't feel the same.

No, I felt nothing for him, he'd killed anything that I felt for him days ago. I turned back to Sam and sighed.

'Because I could understand it, if you did.'

'What?'

'I mean, he's unattainable right? So he's safe-'

'Unattainable? What's that supposed to mean? Like I'm not good enough?'

'No. Ev, be serious,' he said, cocking his head to the side, the exasperation clear in his voice, 'You're so much better than him. You know that!' He smacked me playfully on the arm. 'You see, I have this theory about you.'

'A theory? I'm beginning to get worried about you.'

'I think you blame yourself for your father, for your Gran, the way your mom acts. You think it's all your fault-'

'No, I don't!'

'You do, that's why you push everyone away. That's why you push me away. You feel like you don't deserve to be happy.'

'I-' I didn't deserve to be happy. And I certainly didn't deserve Sam.

'You know I'm right. That's why you like Dexter, because there's no chance, because then you won't hurt him and he won't hurt you. Or, if you're so fixed on him you don't have to get close to someone else.'

I stared at him. 'You really need to quit watching Jeremy Kyle.'

'Make fun if you like, but you know I'm right,' he said, smiling.

I shook my head. 'Ok,' I said, feeling like I should make some sort of confession. 'I did like him...but now I don't,' I added quickly, as I saw the smug smile on his face, 'so that blows your theory right out of the water.'

Sam looked at me, his smile disappearing, his eyebrows knitting together on his forehead. 'Maybe, maybe not.'

'You know I did...but I don't, not now,' I repeated, firmly. And for the first time in ages, I spoke the truth. 'Not how he treated me the other day. I'm not like Cassie.'

Sam was quiet, his eyes studying me for a few moments. 'Good,' he said finally, 'because I think he's a jerk.'

'A jerk, eh?' I said smiling at him, 'Since when did you have an opinion on Dexter?'

Again, he looked at me in silence, his eyes almost searching my face for an answer to a question unspoken.

'And you think I'm weird? You're beginning to freak me out.'

'Just be careful, ok? You're too good for him.'

'I'm always careful.'

He looked back at me with his gentle eyes, but he didn't seem convinced.

After break we made our way to art. I'd got so much going on in my head that every brush stroke on the canvas seemed to be wrong as I tried to transfer my charcoal sketch of the weeping angel from paper to paint. My mind was full of the conversation I'd just had with Sam.

Was Sam right? Was Dexter a distraction, so I wouldn't have to think about getting close to someone else?

I didn't think it was as simple as that. But Sam had made me question myself, he had thrown a new light on my old problems.

I had liked Dexter. A lot. But I'd been trying too hard with him, desperately trying to get him to see me when I didn't know who I was myself. I'd ended up getting lost along the way. Somehow, with all the crap that was my life, I had ended up losing myself.

Surely, when you're supposed to be with someone, it should be easy and you shouldn't have to try that hard?

As my head (or heart) wasn't really into painting I'd already tidied up and put my canvas away when the bell went for dinner. Sam was just finishing up so I told him I'd meet him in the cafeteria as I needed the loo. I grabbed my stuff, headed out the door, and to the nearest toilet just down the corridor.

As I came out of the toilet, Dexter appeared out of nowhere, clutching a bottle of Coke, like some kind of comfort blanket. It was strange to see him in this part of the school as he didn't do Art, but Politics which was way over the other side, in the newer part of the school.

'Hey,' he said.

I scowled at him and walked straight past. How much did he expect me to take? Did he want to have another go at me? Humiliate me even further? Well, it wouldn't work because he couldn't have done it any better than he did after English, the week before. I wasn't in the mood for his silly games.

'Evelyn,' he said, running after me. He reached out and put his hand on my shoulder to stop me.

'What?' I snapped, wrestling my shoulder from him.

'I'm sorry.'

'For what?' Humiliating me? Despising me? The years I have wasted on you?

I spun around to face him, fury blazing inside me.

He dropped his gaze to the floor and shrugged. 'You know.'

'No, I don't know.'

'Oh Evie, don't be like that-'

I jabbed my finger into his chest. He looked at me but didn't move a muscle. 'You don't get to call me Evie-'

'Evelyn...sorry-'

'Yeah, you've said.'

'I shouldn't have done that, the other day, in front of everyone, like that.'

I'd known him for long enough to tell he actually meant it. But what was I supposed to do with that? Wasn't it all a little bit too late?

'And yet you apologise in private?'

'I'm sorry,' he said, looking at me with pleading eyes.

I sighed, my anger turning to pity. 'Dexter, it's too late for apologies.'

'Is everything okay?' It was Sam, striding down the hall, his eyebrows knitted together with concern.

'Yeah,' I said, 'Dexter was just leaving.'

Dexter didn't say a word, but turned and fled down the corridor.

'What was that about?'

'I don't know,' I said. Why would Dexter say sorry to me after everything he'd done? 'But he apologised to me for the other day.'

Sam just clucked. 'Don't you be getting sucked back in, you hear me?'

'What are you, my mother?' I asked, looking up at him and smiling.

'No, I'm better than that,' he said, smiling back.

'But that's not hard is it?'

'I think you might have a point,' he said, putting his arm around me, 'come on, let's grab some dinner.'

We headed off down the stairs to lunch. My mind was a mess, full of anarchic thoughts tumbling around in my head; a chaotic jumble of theories and counter-theories on my life. Why had Dexter apologised? Why had I wasted so much time on him? Was Sam right? Had I used Dexter as a way of keeping others away? Let's face it, Sam had been right in his assessment of me pushing people away, so could he be right now?

And what about Josh?

Josh.

My stomach somersaulted, my heart physically aching as I realised I might never see him again.

'Crap!'

'What? You alright?' said Sam, coming to a standstill on the stairs, almost creating a pile-up as other students grinded to a halt behind us.

'Yeah, I'm fine,' I said, 'I just need.' I said breaking away from him and flying down the stairs, 'I just need to sort something out.'

'Ev!' Sam shouted after me.

'I'm ok, Sam, honest,' I said, not looking back at him, 'Just let Mr Partridge know I've had to go home, tell him I'm ill or something.' And then I was off, cutting my way through the swarms of students making their way to lunch, and out through the doors and into the outside world.

The sun had finally woken up, coating the wet pavements with its warm golden glow as I run out of the school gates and into the centre of town. I rushed down the road to the bus station, my body full of nervous energy. Anxiety was building in me, the restlessness in my soul driving me on.

What if Josh had already left?

What if I never saw him again?

What if I had made the biggest mistake of my life?

Josh

The next morning, I waited until Evie had left, and the house had fallen quiet again, before I carefully let myself out of the front door. Every step felt like I was walking on shards of jagged glass. It wouldn't have surprised me if I had looked back and seen a trail of blood on the floor.

I blended into the crowds of people, trying desperately not to turn back, to not change my mind. My head was telling me to run, to get away as far as possible and not come back, for her sake, but my heart, my heart was slowly killing me as it tried to get me to turn around, and drag me back to her house, and back to her.

When I didn't listen, my heart started screaming at me, burning for her, but what good was it? We couldn't be together, not when I was a freak with a death sentence hanging over me. I could feel the invisible chord, that anchored me to her, pulling tightly around me, suffocating me, when I ventured too far away from her.

I would have to get used to that feeling.

I had to stay away; Death could not win.

I got back to my apartment but there was a gaping hole beside me. Death had known exactly what She was doing when She had left me for dead; my body, although still battered and bruised, was now healing but my closeness to Evie during my recovery was like giving an addict drugs, my body was aching for her, trembling and in shock without her.

I dragged myself to the bathroom, peeling off Dan's clothes like a snake shedding its old skin, peeling away Evie's scent, the ghost of her.

I looked over my shoulder and into the mirror at my wings folded tightly into my skin. They had healed well but still simmered with pain, especially when I thought about her.

I stepped into the shower, hoping to wash her away, to stop the scent of her on my skin driving me mad.

I was doomed with her, destroyed without.

It didn't work; I couldn't get her out of my head, the way she moved, the curl of her lips, the feel of her skin.

I got dressed and went into the dining room, switching on the laptop to try and distract myself. I knew Death wouldn't let me go easily - that much She had proven to me already - I could not die when I wanted to, only when She had finished with me. I needed to find Hyperion, needed to finish it, so She would let me go, then my torment would be over. I couldn't afford to listen to anymore of his seductive lies.

I looked at the news reports of the devastation left behind by Hyperion; the death toll was now at six hundred and thirty-three, and I grieved in my heart for every single life lost because of Hyperion's ego. But no matter how much I looked at the laptop or tried to forget Evie, she forced herself into my mind until I could think of nothing else.

I couldn't just walk out of her life, disappear like a ghost, I needed to say goodbye, she deserved that at least.

I headed for the door. I'd sit her down, say goodbye, then I'd be able to concentrate on what I needed to do; ending my life.

It was the best way. The only way.

She had to forget about me.

Evie

The journey on the bus home was torture. I think we hit every set of traffic lights in the neighbourhood. I kept looking at my phone, checking to see how many minutes had gone by, and how long I'd been on the bus. The minutes were racing by, but the bus seemed to be crawling along.

What if he'd gone already? How would I even find him again? I knew virtually nothing about him. And yet, it didn't matter, because I *did* know him. Deep down, in my soul, there was a place set aside for him. With all the crap that was my life, and the mess of thoughts rattling around in my head, there was only one thing that I was completely sure of; I had to stop him leaving. I had to put up a fight because I couldn't just let him walk out of my life.

I jumped off the bus and ran down the road, hoping that he was still holed up in my bedroom, that Cassie and Dan's antics had stopped him from leaving. The fire in my belly was roaring now, driving me forwards, despite the agony in my lungs.

I got to the front door. The house seemed dead, but the fire refused to be put out until I knew for certain he was gone. I flung open the door, not caring if Cassie or Dan were there, I'd deal with that later. I raced upstairs, threw open my bedroom door and...

He was gone.

My heart broke, splintered into thousands of tiny pieces, like a glass thrown to the floor.

I slumped onto the bed. I had let the only good thing in my life go.

How would I ever find him again?

'Hey, you okay?'

I looked up, not quite believing he was actually still there, standing in the doorway. My breath caught in my throat, my breathing quickened. I didn't dare look at his eyes, I didn't want to give the game away, didn't want to scare him.

I let my eyes linger upon the small sliver of a tattoo wing and dagger peeking out from under his grey shirt. I just wanted to wrap my arms around him.

I needed to get a grip and slow myself down. What if I'd read it all wrong?

I bit my lip, trying not to give in and look at his face. I couldn't blow this one and final chance. 'I'm fine, really, I just...'

Too late, my eyes locked onto his and my heart skipped a beat. My legs were trembling, even though I was sitting down. What if I blew this? What if he didn't want me? My stomach turned over but I didn't think that it had anything to do with skipping dinner.

'I'm sorry for running out on you this morning-'

'It's ok-'

'No, it's not.'

I couldn't move my eyes from his, I couldn't think straight and my words just tumbled from my mouth. 'It just scared me, being so close to you.'

'I'm that bad, I scared you?' he said, stepping into the room and shutting the door behind him.

The look of horror on his face ripped me in two. 'No.'

'I would never hurt you. And I'm sorry if I've ever scared you-'

'I know,' I said, standing up and turning to face him, 'I like you Josh, a lot, but my heads all messed up. I don't know who I am anymore, and I don't trust myself to get things right. I don't know if you like me, or if you don't, and now I'm rabbling even though I'm trying to be really cool and act like it's not a big deal. I think, I get the impression that you like me too, I don't know why but-'

'I do.'

'What?'

'Like you.'

Heat suddenly coursed through my body, and I knew I was blushing. 'Even though I left this morning without saying goodbye? And I told you to leave?'

'It was understandable-'

'Maybe...My life...my life is a mess right now, and Cassie, my mother, has this habit of jumping into bed with a guy every time something bad happens and I don't want to do that. I don't want be like her.'

'And?'

'I'm not. I know I'm not. But it took a good friend, and thinking I'd never see you again, to make me see that. I'm nothing like Cassie, you have to believe me-'

'It sounds like you're trying to convince yourself-'

'No,' I said, shaking my head, 'I'm not.' I walked over to him. I was standing only centimetres away from him and when I looked at him the world didn't exist, there was only me and him, in nothing but time and space.

The air was almost fizzing around us, a pulse of what? Attraction? I knew that's how I felt. I just longed for him to put his arms around me and kiss me. To me, it was like we were positive and negative electrons and protons being brought together by the force of physics; natural and completely unstoppable. I had never felt like this before and I wanted to grab on to it with both hands and never let that feeling go.

We looked at each other, not wanting to move, not wanting to leave the moment, afraid of what was going to happen next. We were on the edge of something, and, I knew, I was about to fall. I knew that I shouldn't do what I was about to, but also, that I was still going to do it anyway.

And it felt delicious.

'I feel like I've known you forever...even though I don't know you at all. Does that make sense?' Was I saying too much? Was I going to destroy the moment, like I usually did? But my words would not listen to my concern and instead, kept tumbling from my mouth. 'I've got a feeling, that I just can't shake, don't want to shake, that I've met you before.'

'Maybe, in some time, some place, we *have* met before.'

'Do you believe in parallel universes? Maybe in one of those we were lovers.'

'So what happens now?' he asked, reaching up to brush a stray hair from my face.

His touch was electric and I couldn't stand it any longer. I leaned forward, my eyes still locked onto his, and I kissed him.

I pushed him backwards, the door banged shut, my eyes closed, our lips locked, our bodies combined as one, and I didn't care at that moment who knew.

Time had simply stopped.

And then Cassie was banging on my door. 'You okay? You're back early?'

Reluctantly I let our lips part, but I couldn't stop looking at his beautiful eyes. 'Yes,' I said, trying to contain my breathlessness, not sure how I would explain it away if she came in. 'Free period,' I said, praying that she'd go away. I couldn't talk, didn't want to talk.

Josh brushed my face with his hand before placing it on my neck. His touch was like fire. He leaned towards me and rested his forehead on mine, trying to regain control. It was almost impossible to fight the urge to kiss him again.

'Oh, okay then. Me and Dan are going out later, alright if you get your own tea?'

'Yeah,' I said. My voice was shaky, betraying me to anyone that would listen, but luckily for me at that moment, Cassie did what she always does, and didn't listen.

'Don't wait up,' she said, and I heard her footsteps trailing off downstairs.

'So, what *do* we do now?' I asked, shivering as he run his hand through my hair.

'Whatever you want,' he replied, pulling me to him again.

There was a slight flicker on my subconscious somewhere, a little image of a strange sort of darkness, an emptiness, like although he was physically there in front of me, somewhere in time, he'd been taken from me. And inside I grieved for my loss, even though he was still standing there before me.

Josh

I'd gone back to say goodbye, but the battle was lost as soon as she kissed me.

I am too weak to resist.

My body erupted into flames, my wings felt like they're going to burst out of my back, but I didn't care, didn't want it to end. I thought I was going to die, consumed by my desire.

I didn't want to let her go. Ever. This moment had to last forever.

Time seemed to stop, and for that moment there was only the two of us, lost in each other, in the heat of our desire. If I had died at that moment, consumed by the flames of that desire, it would have been a blissful death.

But everything comes to an end, this time with a bang on the door, and our lips parted, although the fire still burned deep within us, I could feel it scorching my soul. I rested my forehead on hers, tried to get control of my breathing, tried to fight the need to kiss her again.

I love you, I said to her, although the words didn't leave my mouth.

'So, what *do* we do now?' she asked.

'Whatever you want,' I said, pulling her towards me again. I thought about pulling back, running away, because I shouldn't have been there, it was too dangerous, but I couldn't. I was hooked. The pain that Death had promised me, wasn't as severe now, dimming under the brightness of Evie's touch, and any pain that I did feel, I welcomed, because I knew I was alive. But it was also strange that now, when I touched her, I didn't see the images of her life anymore, just felt the simmering pain.

That's what she did to me. She made me lose my mind.

She pulled away. 'Are we really going to do this?' she asked. 'If that's what you want?'

I looked into her eyes. They were so beautiful, dazzling, like her aura. I didn't answer her question with words but instead placed a tender kiss on her lips. Soon we were lying on the bed, our bodies and lips entwined as the rain pounded outside, the street lamps glistening through the windows, as the darkness fell. And I felt like I'd come home.

Eventually, our lips parted. 'I have to go,' I said.

She gave me those pleading eyes and if she'd have asked me to give her the world in that one moment, I'd have done it. 'Really? Have I put you off already?'

I smiled at her, running the tip of my thumb over her lips. 'No. That could never happen. There's something I've got to do. But I'll be back. I promise.'

As soon as I was alone I broke out my wings, let the pain take me into the darkness, let it cleanse me. I was shining, brought back to life by Evie. Once the pain had subsided, I stretched them out, feeling every feather bristle against the wind, every bone and connecting tissue move. I was alive.

I soared into the clear night's sky, the heavens sparkling around me, and for the first time I saw the true beauty of it. Before long the never-ending darkness sought me out, wound its fingers around my body and She came to me, like a mistress in the night.

'Josh,' She sighed, 'I thought we'd been through how this works. You can't outwit me. I thought you were much cleverer than that.'

'You pushed me into a corner,' I said, to the darkness snaking around my body, 'and I wanted out, but I know now that I have no control over that.'

Her cold cackle cut through the darkness. She appeared before me, thin strands of the universe covering her body. 'No, Josh, you can't die until I say. You should've known that already.'

'I do, I did.'

She smiled and glided over to me, the tendrils of darkness barely covering her curves and yet, She did nothing for me.

'I sense a change in you,' She said, regarding me with Her black eyes. She leaned forward and cradled my face in Her hands, placing a cold kiss on my lips.

Her iciness penetrated deep within me, slithering down to my soul, but it couldn't pierce its shell for a new light burned there.

'Have you learnt your lesson now?'

I nodded. 'But please, I beg you, don't ever use Evie again, I will do whatever you ask, but please, leave her out of it.'

'Oh, Josh, you are so sentimental. It's quite adorable,' She said, patting me on the head. 'The trouble is, Evelyn is part of this now, and I can't change that, but if you do what needs to be done, she won't get hurt. Simple as that.'

'But she will get hurt, won't she, when you finally take me?'

'Hyperion already has the first relic because of your incompetence. All those extra dead souls, because of you. You must stop him, kill him, before he re-unites all the relics. And remember, Evie's life depends on you.'

Epilogue

Josh

The coffee machine purred as it spewed out the black gold, delicious tendrils of the bitter sweet aroma reaching out to embrace the morning, pulling me from the dream that was the night before. I looked out of the window and saw the dark clouds gathering on the horizon. I knew it couldn't stay like that forever, that Death awaited, and Hyperion.

I turned away, my mind recoiling from reality, seeking refuge in the memories of the night. I could still see her sleeping beside me, her arm draped across my chest, a smile dancing upon her lips. And it felt so right, like a tailored coat placed back upon my shoulders. God made her for me and it feels so comfortable being with her, like we had always been together.

And then I awoke to sunlight fanning the room and the sound of morning; car doors slamming, the trundling of traffic and the excited screams of the kids making their way to school. Evie was lying on her side, perched upon her elbow, her face glowing above me, her smile as bright as the sunshine outside.

'Hey you,' she said, stroking my lips with her thumb. Her touch, although light as a feather, penetrated deep within me, like an electric shock. I lay there, unable to move as the electric pulsed through my veins. It had been so long since I had slept so peacefully or normally during the night that I almost didn't want to be awake and yet I wanted to spend forever in that moment, just looking at her face.

But darkness invaded my thoughts and I knew, sometime in the future, I would have to leave her, for good. Who was I kidding thinking that being with her was even possible? How could I lead her on that way, knowing that it could only add up to trouble and hurt?

'Come on,' she said, leaning forwards to plant a kiss on my forehead, 'I need coffee.' And as easy as that I was sucked back in again, unable to leave, intoxicated by the smell of strawberry and cherry blossom. The physical pain of being with her, although throbbing throughout my body, was now part of me, part of us and it was as addictive as she was.

The honeyed vocals of Michael Hutchence soared from the speakers in the living room, bringing me back to the present. I grabbed the coffee mugs from the machine and strode into the living room but stopped dead as I turned the corner. Evie was swaying in the middle of the room, millions of dust motes flittering around her like tiny butterflies. The warm sun streamed in from the window, enveloping her in a golden mist which made her look heavenly, like she was the Angel. A lump caught in my throat as my eyes traced the contour of her silhouette rocking gently to the music. She raised her right arm slowly into the air and her ebony hair cascaded down the back of her neck like a waterfall of cocaine. A certain kind of sadness ripped me apart in that moment, the kind that physically hurts right in the bottom of your stomach.

I was hurtling towards a collision, like a runaway train.

I fell back onto the door frame, defeated. My heart oscillating between ecstasy and misery.

Her left hand slowly moved over her the top of her leg and onto her hip. My eyes lingered upon the small sliver of pale flesh exposed as her white tee-shirt was displaced by the movement. I could feel an uncontrollable heat rising through my body as my eyes devoured that small slice of skin as it was removed from view then exposed again. Eventually my gaze was torn away as she lifted her arms to run her fingers through her hair, revealing the arch of her neck.

She turned, dropping her hair back down around her shoulders, a wide smile spreading across her face as her eyes locked on to mine. She continued to dance in front of me, her face alive with happiness, her eyes not moving from mine and shining with such an intensity that set me on fire. My body was aching for her.

There was no going back, for either of us.

And as I stood there, fixed to the spot, I knew that I should find the strength to walk away, pull back and save her the pain.

But she had my soul in the palm of her hands.

The pain of being close to her crucifies me but it also makes me feel alive, more alive than in the hundreds of years of being an angel. The beautiful pain and electrifying pleasure of being with her is something that I can't give it up. I'm not strong enough.

And then she was in front of me, dazzling like the stars. She took the mugs from my trembling hands and put them down on the table. She turned and grabbed me, dragging me right into the living room and I'm powerless under her touch. Electricity is surging through my body, scaring me and thrilling me in equal measure. She lets my hands drop and dances around me, completely unaware of the power she has over me.

And my heart starts to break apart as she pulls me in.

'Come on!' she pleaded, 'dance with me!' I shot a glimpse at the door, knowing that that was it; I should leave.

Then the music changed, and there was a melody in the air made of guitar and saxophone. Her arms slipped around my waist and I cannot breath. I cannot think. I felt her warmth as she moved in close. I let my hand trace the small of her back, down to the waistband of her shorts.

If I were a human, I'd probably be heading for Hell.

But as I'm an Angel of Death, it doesn't matter, I'll dance through the flames.

There's a storm coming, I can feel it in my bones, and like a ship with no sail, I'm heading straight for it.

I smiled and placed my other hand at the back of her head, pulling her in to me.

And my heart finally smashes in to a million pieces.

And they can never tear us apart, she sings to me.

But they will, I say, silently.

###

Thank you for taking the time to read Everlong, I hope you enjoyed it!

Nikki xx

About the Author

If I were a song, I'd be Doomsday by Kasabian.

If I were a film, I'd like to be one that has Christoph Waltz in it, or Al Pacino. Either would make me happy.

If I were a Boxset, I'd want it to be The Sopranos.

I love walking in the rain, especially if I've got nowhere to go.

Winter's my favourite time of year, it fits me, unlike summer when everyone thinks you should be happy. Happiness doesn't just appear because the suns out, life doesn't work like that.

I love reading - Harry Potter, Twilight, Memoirs of a Geisha, Da Vinci Code are all in my top ten. Don't make me choose one. That would be like asking me to choose between my children. It just wouldn't happen.

Discover other titles by Nikki Morgan at Amazon:

Blackthorn - Revenge of the Dragon Rider, a dark
dystopian fantasy set in the near future
http://www.amazon.co.uk/Blackthorn-Revenge-Dragon-
Nikki-Morgan-ebook/dp/B008QP4V2E

Book Two of the Everlong Trilogy will be available soon.

Connect with me online:

https://www.facebook.com/NikkiMorganauthor
http://nikkimorgan.weebly.com
http://www.amazon.co.uk/Nikki-Morgan/e/B008RB2AMK

Made in the USA
Charleston, SC
05 October 2014